IMPRINTED

The Imprinted Trilogy, Book 1

Brooke Stemme

Cover and Interior Elements by: sparklestroke and dadangkap from Gambar Dadang Kap, through Canva

Second Edition

Paperback ISBN: 979-8-9897428-4-4

eBook ISBN: 979-8-9897428-5-1

To Gabby, my first writing friend

Chapter 1

Every morning Kierian trades the confines of his clan's enclave for the four walls of an antique store. At least in the store he can control the prices. It would be more tolerable if he could control who he worked shifts with. Knowing who he's working with today makes Kierian's stomach twist.

He only needs make it through midday, then he can leave. As long as Pryor is overcharging and persuading customers to buy more than they need, Kierian doesn't have to worry. He can stand at the register and type in whatever Pryor says. It's when Pryor disappears into the storage room attached to the back of the store that Kierian's conscience starts to burn. He could find out what goes on back there if he wanted to. Pryor has offered, but Kierian has always declined. Today won't be the day he changes his mind.

The first thing Kierian notices is blood on the handle of the back door. He recoils from it. It's fresh, he can smell it. His stomach turns over, fangs pushing against his lip as he averts his gaze. Careful to avoid any other possible spots, Kierian knocks on the door. "Can someone let me in?"

There's a clattering from the other side of the door before Pryor answers. "Go around. I hope you didn't forget your keys! I'll help you out front in a little bit, just give me a few more minutes, will you?"

Kierian lingers for a moment. The only sounds he can hear are light scuffles and Pryor's muttering, too quiet to make out. If it were anyone else, he could assume Pryor was reorganizing the storage room and move on. That would be too easy of an answer this time. Kierian knows what he is, what both of them are. Every day is too real for him to forget. But as much as Kierian hates what he is, Pryor revels in it. Kierian steps away from the back door, trying to force every sound he catches into the category of "normal" and not "possibly human" coming from the back room.

Coming around to the front of the antique store, Kierian fishes the key out from his pocket. There's no blood on this handle. That, at least, is a positive sign. The bells above the door jingle as he steps inside and flips the sign to open. He crosses to the far side of the room, positioning himself behind the checkout counter. As long as he shows up to work, and as long as Pryor's problems don't become his, everything will be fine - fine enough that he doesn't have to think about it.

Kierian glances over his shoulder at the curtain separating the store from the back room. He can hear Pryor rustling among the random accumulation of objects, but the room itself is mostly left to Kierian's imagination. He checks his hands. They're clean. Cold, though pressing his palms against the counter does little to combat that. He just can't get his imagination to settle.

Pryor showed him the shop the very first day he worked here. Rattled, grieving, and more than a little angry, Kierian knew from the start they weren't going to be friends. Pryor's insistence on becoming a part of the clan only stirred Kierian's hatred further. That, the pink stains on his shirt, and the faint scent of iron Pryor never bothered to fully clean off his sleeves.

"We can't live forever but we can get close," Kierian mutters, remembering Pryor's words then adding his own. "It's not worth it to pay that price, not with someone else's blood."

The bells above the door ring, pulling Kierian from his thoughts. He looks up, watching the girl come into the shop. Dark, curly hair frames her face, the hem of her sweatshirt pulling up in one corner to reveal a muddy yellow shirt. She must be about the same age as him. Her eyes scan the store rapidly, the motion at odds with the rest of her appearance. She steps inside the store just enough for the door to close without hitting her. Kierian frowns, but before he can say anything, she's already speaking.

"Has a girl been in here today? Short sleeves, jeans?" she asks.

Kierian blinks at her for a moment before he can respond. "We just opened. You're the first one in today."

She takes a deep, shaky breath. "Can you look out for her? This is the first place I can think of that she might go." She doesn't break eye contact with him.

"Sure," Kierian says. "But I'm not sure..."

"Her name is Vivian," she says, her words coming quickly. "She's a few years younger than me, same dark hair but straighter. I can't remember what she was wearing today, but..."

She's cut off by a voice from the back room. "Kierian! Are you selling anything?" There's a metallic thud from something back there hitting the ground.

Kierian's gut twists but he forces himself to smile at the girl. The last thing he wants is for Pryor to come out here. The longer she's here asking questions the more danger she puts herself in. There's just no way to tell her that.

"If she comes in, I'll let you know," Kierian says. "Can I get your name?"

She nods. "I'm Cassie," she says. "Thank you so much. Please let her know that I'm looking for her if you see her. You can tell her I'll be back here later, or at home, but I have to keep looking..."

Kierian only hears part of what she says. The curtain to the back room rustles, drawing his eye. His attention shifts from Cassie even as she keeps talking. Not a few moments later, Pryor comes through the curtain. Kierian can see his fangs half-extended, the cuffs of his sleeves rolled up, and eyes on Cassie.

"Sounds like there may be something going on out here," Pryor says. "Can I help answer any questions?"

"You don't need to come out here," Kierian says, glaring at Pryor for just a moment. His tone dips lower, hoping to get across an unspoken message to Pryor to leave this girl alone.

"Whatever help you need..."

"Get out." Kierian cuts Pryor off sharply. It feels like something rushes out from himself, like Kierian can protect her. Cassie may be a stranger, but he's no stranger to Pryor's hobbies. If he can keep Pryor from hurting her...

"I'd have done this sooner if I knew how you'd react," Pryor says. He smiles, fangs bared. He nods once in Cassie's direction. "Look at her."

Kierian's first instinct is to distrust everything Pryor says. But when he sees her, Kierian's stomach drops. She stares back at him. Her eyes are a wide dark brown, mouth slightly parted. They've explained what this is. An imprint. Having someone explain a feeling and experiencing it himself is something totally different. Extending out from him is a tangible connection. He can't see it, but it draws him toward Cassie. He's not quite convinced she's breathing.

"Cassie?" Kierian says.

She takes a quick breath, stepping backward. She shakes her head, but her eyes don't leave Kierian. It takes all his strength to keep his expression neutral. If she really did imprint on him, they're in more trouble than she could possibly know.

"Isn't it nice to really meet each other?" Pryor says. "It's so much nicer not to have to wear a mask." Shock is the only thing that keeps Kierian's building rage at Pryor in check.

"What's happening?" Cassie says. The worry and passion she had when she walked into the shop is gone. In its place is curiosity tinged with what Kierian can only imagine is fear.

"How sweet," Pryor starts. "You know..."

Kierian points toward the back of the room, turning the full force of his attention on Pryor. "Get out," Kierian says again. Pryor makes no attempt to move. He just stands there, infuriatingly. But at least he's not looking at her.

The bells above the door ring as it slams shut. She's gone. There's a sharp pull out the door where Cassie was just a moment ago, but it's the crimson blood stains on Pryor's shirt and the shock of these last few minutes that threaten to draw out Kierian's fangs.

"I said get out of my sight!" Kierian shouts the words, balling his hands into fists. "Get back to whatever you were doing before but leave things out here alone."

"Or what?" Pryor says. He sneers, his fangs clearly visible. "What will you do if I refuse? I run things around here, fledgling. If anything, you should thank me. You're one step closer to becoming what you're meant to be."

Pryor doesn't move, but pain lances through Kierian. It only lasts for a second, but Kierian can feel the full force of it through to core. It sends him stumbling backward, his knees giving out as his hands flail for a grip on the counter. He holds fast to the wood grain, his knuckles white. With something solid underneath him, he can focus on two things: the temptation to fight Pryor the way the other vampire would like him to, and the panicked tugging from Cassie. His imprint. It's the acknowledgement of those two words that extinguishes the fight in him.

His imprint. The one thing he promised himself he would never let happen. Now he's done the same thing that was done to him. As long as he lives, she won't be able to unsee the world that's been revealed to her.

A hand closes around Kierian's jaw, forcing his head up. Pryor towers over him, a satisfied smile on his face. "Still trying to resist it?" Pryor asks. There's a mockery to his tone as he leans in close. "You'll come around, I'm sure of it. We all do eventually. You know the clan's rules. You need to bring her in. She's yours for now, but then she'll become one of us. You'll make her one of us."

Kierian grips the counter harder. The pressure in his gut is almost unbearable, but he keeps himself in check. He grits his teeth, his gaze not moving from Pryor. "Did you forget the part where she has a choice?" Kierian says. "Where she gets to decide her own fate?" He phrases it as a question, but they both know it isn't one.

Pryor pushes his face hard to the side, Kierian's nose colliding with the edge of the counter. "There's much worse than that coming for you," Pryor says. "Trust me on that if it's the only time you believe me. She is ours now. That is all your doing. Now it's up to you what kind of role she plays. If you do refuse, just know I'll gladly be the first to volunteer to ensure both of you pay."

Kierian drags a sleeve across his nose, catching the droplets of blood that have fallen there. None of the words he wants to say will earn him anything else but more spilled blood. He'd like to avoid bleeding out here.

Pryor shrugs, his grin one of amusement now. "Is that all you've got?" he says, laughing. "Your first one. Too bad you were the one she was looking at, otherwise it would have been a lot more fun."

Kierian grips the edge of the counter, pulling himself upright. He fights to keep himself steady, to make sure Pryor doesn't feel the need to slam his face into the counter again. "You think every person who walks in here gets to be a part of your game?" Kierian says. "That the moment they walk through this door, their blood might be yours?" His voice is quiet, but the words are barbed.

Pryor's smile fades. "What I do is nothing more than tradition. You're too young to respect that, though, aren't you?"

"I don't need to chase immortality. You know it can't keep you alive forever, no matter whose blood it is you take." The words sound better in his head than out loud.

Pryor shakes his head, turning his back to Kierian. "You're young. Like I said, you'll come around to it. There's your first imprint, then there's your first real taste of blood. Once you know what the real thing is like, nothing's quite the same again."

The beads click as Pryor passes through the curtain to the back room, muttering something under his breath. Kierian glares at the space Pryor no longer occupies. It takes all his strength to walk across the shop, feeling the imprint shift as he moves. He flips the store's sign to closed and locks the door. He gets a few odd looks from the street, but Kierian just shrugs. If he has to try and figure all this out, he's not going to bother selling antiques as he does it. As soon as he's back behind the counter, he slumps to the floor.

"What have I done?" Kierian whispers the words, his face in his hands. There's a reason he never wanted to create an imprint. He's been careful not to reveal himself to anyone, on purpose or by accident. He let his guard down in a critical moment. She was in danger, and he had to do something about it. He didn't realize what had happened until it was too late. Imprinting on him means he's pulled back the veil of this city so she can see it as it really is.

The shop is strangely quiet. The front door is still locked, but it's possible Pryor could have left out the back. It's also possible he might have left something behind. There's no excitement in Kierian's movements as he moves toward the back room. He pulls the curtain back in one sharp movement, steeling himself for what he might find.

Kierian's eyes dart away from the variety of items on the floor, most of them tinted with some shade of crimson, from deep red to a dirty brown. Chairs are pushed against the wall next to mostly empty bookshelves. One side table furnishes the room. The only light in the room comes from where Kierian pulled the curtain back. What catches his attention is the bright red handprint on the back door. It's fresh, like the blood on Pryor's shirt. There was someone else back here. Kierian's stomach clenches at that idea. Her sister might have even been here, and he never knew. He never bothered to check. Maybe Pryor is right about some things. He might speak out against tradition, but what is he doing to change it?

"I can't stand around and do nothing," Kierian mutters. Kierian's only plan of action is half-baked and questionable at best, but if he can't trust Pryor, the best way to avoid suspicion is to follow the same pattern he does every day as if nothing is any different. Careful to avoid as much blood as possible, he crosses the back room and peers out the door. As far as he can tell, the alley is empty. Kierian looks around for a moment longer then steps out of the store. The door clicks shut behind him. A dark set of crimson footprints follow him, a stain on the concrete. And so, Kierian heads toward the place he never has, or will, call his home.

Chapter 2

CASSIE CAN'T GET THE scene to stop replaying in her head. His face changed. No matter how hard she tries to convince herself it didn't happen, she saw his face change. His skin got paler and the roots of his hair turned a silvery color. The tips of his two teeth were too long, and his eyes - two slits with veins of yellow like a reptile.

The bells on the door alert everyone to her escape. Cassie's gut wrenches as she passes over the threshold of the store, but she doesn't look back. She can't look back. If her eyes are playing tricks on her, the easiest rebuttal would be to look back and realize she's made a complete fool out of herself. If she turns back and everything still looks the same, if those same unnatural features are still staring back at her... Cassie does the only thing she can think to do - put as much distance between herself and that shop as possible.

Cassie gets as far away as her body will let her. By the time she finally stops, her lungs ache, her feet hurt, and her side is screaming in pain. She leans up against the nearest wall to catch her breath. As she takes in her surroundings, her lack of familiarity with this sector of the city isn't what worries her the most. First, she has a feeling she's supposed to go somewhere. Not a premonition, a physical tug. It's as if someone tied a rope around her waist and is pulling. Second, nothing looks normal anymore. Kierian couldn't have changed his appearance in a normal way as quickly as it happened. But all around her are people that don't look like people. They're something else. Walking past her are colored veins, insect-like eyes, and fur. Those are the only things she can wrap her mind around.

In a city, there's only supposed to be people walking by. Hundreds of people all the time, but people. The height, posture, and even bone structure of some of them are very much not normal. She pinches herself but nothing happens. She's not quite sure what's more terrifying - that her sister is gone, there are unnatural things walking by like everything is fine, or that there are normal people mixed in who don't seem to be having the same reaction she is.

"This can't be real," Cassie whispers to herself. "This can't be real."

There's only one place she can think of going. She takes a few steps forward, toward home, the one place she assumes can't change. But as she does, that physical tugging grows tighter. It tugs her in a different direction. She tries to ignore it, but no matter how hard she tries to focus on home it keeps getting tighter.

Cassie looks down. She puts a hand on her stomach but there's nothing there, nothing she can see anyway. If it was only Kierian, even if it was only those two in the shop, she might be able to convince herself it was panic. If she were dreaming, she'd have woken up by now. All she has now is this strange sensation she can't get to go away. There has to be something at the end of it. She has no earthly idea what that might be.

Cassie remembers the hunger in the eyes of the second face she saw in the store. "Do I really want to find that?" she whispers. A she forces herself to look, she realizes that hunger was not isolated to the one man. There are others who glance at her with a similar coldness in their smiles, one that would devour her if they got close enough. She's not safe here. She might not be safe anywhere, but she's certainly not safe here.

"Where do I go?" She can hardly hear her thoughts over the roaring of blood in her ears. The thought of running only makes her lungs ache more. She can't go back to the antique store. Her whole being rejects that idea. Cassie could go home and wait. That seems like the logical answer, the most reasonable place Vivian would go if she got the change. Blood on her sister's pillowcase and her shattered bedroom window flash through Cassie's mind. Whatever happened, Cassie can't believe her sister left of her own free will. If she got away, Cassie might know where she'd run. But without knowing who or why... If she can't trust what she's seeing, if there's a chance Vivian is seeing the same things, no one is going to believe her. Cassie can't wait for the world to return to normal. She has to be the one to find her sister.

Her gaze drifts down to her stomach again. There's nothing obvious that suggests to her there is in fact a rope tied around her. But even if she can't see this rope, she can still feel it. So, against her better judgment, she closes her eyes. As she does, tension pulls against her. It's light enough it doesn't force her to move but it's strong enough to suggest she does. It still doesn't feel like a great idea, but it's the only lead she has.

Cassie focuses on memories of her sister. She imagines sitting at a small round table with dolls in white chairs and teacups filled with lemonade, a dimpled smile. Crimson flashes in her vision again. Although Cassie's heartbeat spikes, she pushes the vision away. She's back to late nights sitting on a bed too small for the both of them and their whispered conversations filling the room. She can almost feel their goodnight hug from the last time she saw Vivian, just last night. Cassie takes a deep, shaky breath and tries to funnel all those memories into the strange tension that's wrapped around her. Whatever's changed, maybe she can use it to help.

"Vivian?" she whispers. "Please help me find her." There's a faint pulse in response. Cassie's eyes snap open. She can't explain any of it. Nothing looks the same as it did when she woke up this morning, but nothing was the way it was supposed to be when the sun came up and found her sister taken. If there's any possibility this thing can show her where Vivian is, she's going to take it.

Cassie weaves her way through the streets, letting the rope guide her. There's a tension she carries in her body, beyond the invisible sense of one the one she can't figure out. There's a slight downturn to her mouth, a focused stare ahead, and a tightness of her muscles in her shoulders as she walks. The further she goes, the more her legs start to ache. Despite that, though, she can't get the image of her sister or Kierian out of her mind.

Cassie hesitates as she the force she's been following shifts direction. "If Vivian is moving," she whispers. "Maybe she's okay." She doesn't let herself consider any other possibility.

It's her sister's hazel eyes, a smile so full of life and joy, she tries to picture on. An unwanted dread eats away at Cassie's thoughts. It's bouncy curls and the timid wringing of Vivian's hands when she's nervous that Cassie focuses on. That and trying to reach the end of the invisible rope tied to her.

As the sun dips closer to the horizon, a bit of relief comes to Cassie. She's nearing the end of it. The tension and length of it feels within reach, not like a bungee cord that could snap at any moment. She turns down a dimly lit street and her heart sinks. She's tugged onward but there's nowhere to go. The street is a dead end. Three walls surround her, and the only other direction is back the way she came. Her new instinct is telling her she's close, so close, and yet there's nothing but brick walls.

"Where are you?" Cassie whispers. As she does, she feels one ripple along the invisible rope. The ripple comes back to her, pulling her a step closer to the far wall. She narrows her eyes at the wall and tries again.

"Where are you?"

Again, the same ripple goes out and returns to her. She continues to approach the far wall. Wandering the city streets in the dark isn't her ideal plan. She might as well take her chances with this first.

Cassie approaches the far wall, stopping just a few feet away from it. She raises her hand, pressing her palm to it. Her fingers disappear through it in the same moment a hand closes around her wrist and pulls. Cassie tumbles through the wall, her pulse spiking and adrenaline running through her veins. She gasps, her eyes scanning the space rapidly in the dim light. Laughter fills the air, a hand still tight around her wrist. Deep muddy eyes with only a black slit stare back at her, a mouth turned up in one corner with two teeth protruding over his lower lip. He's not Vivian. He looks more like Kierian.

He holds her tightly for a moment longer then lets her go. Cassie remains frozen in place. She doesn't dare speak. She's not sure what would come out of her mouth if she did.

"You know someone here?" the man says. He glances back at a full table, the rest of them sitting. "It's not me."

"I..." Cassie starts.

"Girl! Here."

A voice booms from across the room and she finally has a moment to take in her surroundings. It's a bar. Tables, chairs, and low lights fill the room. Her eyes skim over the particulars of the inhabitants, some of them still snickering or whispering in her direction. She makes eye contact with the hulking figure behind the bar on the far side of the space. He's talking to her, there's no doubt in Cassie's mind. The gray, hulking figure staring at her doesn't calm her.

"Taking away all our fun, Olgber?" says the man who grabbed her. "I was just asking who she was here for. We could help." It's the tone of his voice, and the not so hidden sneer, that propels Cassie toward the bar. She can feel the stares as she walks deeper into the room. It's those stares that keep her from turning and running out. It doesn't matter where she goes if they can follow her. If she runs, they can follow her.

Cassie stops in front of the bar, glancing at the door just past it. It has to lead somewhere. The shadow looming over her demands her attention, though. She has to bend her head back in order to meet those large, deep eyes. Her only relief is in the fact they're not slits.

"Girl?" he asks.

Cassie waits for a beat, but he doesn't say anything else. "Yes."

"Looking for something?"

Cassie hesitates, her throat dry. He narrows his eyes, though only his top lids move when he blinks. He turns slowly over his shoulder toward the door off to the side of the bar, then back to Cassie.

"Looking for someone?" he says, rephrasing the question.

Cassie presses her lips together, her pulse rushing in her ears. There's not a single thing she can think of to say that could possibly turn out well for her in this situation. Whatever this situation is.

It's then, with unexpected speed, that a thick hand darts out from behind the bar taking hold of her. She's not entirely sure what leaves her mouth as her stomach drops and she's lifted swiftly off the ground, her feet are dangling in mid-air. Her call for help gets stuck in her throat, her whole world tilting.

Chapter 3

KIERIAN LEANS AGAINST THE main hallway of his clan's enclave. Eyes closed, he frowns as he feels what he assumes to be the distance between him and Cassie shrinking. The whole point of coming here was to prevent his clan from getting suspicious so he could figure out what to do. She wasn't supposed to come find him. But how could she have known that?

Kierian can still remember what it was like to be human. It's only been a year since everything changed. His imprint then abandoned him until it was convenient. He told himself he would be different, but so far everything he's tried so hard not to become is exactly what he's turning out to be. Despite what he told himself, he's making the same choices.

With no warning, the imprint creates a crushing pressure on his chest. He stumbles forward and slams into the opposite wall. It comes on so suddenly he can hardly catch himself, pain spiking through his wrists.

"Cassie."

He's not sure if her name leaves his mouth, if it's a thought, or an instinct. There's only one thing on his mind: she's in danger.

He pushes off the wall, quickly moving down the hall to the door, back into the bar. It slams hard into the wall as he bursts through it. All eyes are on Cassie, the bartender holding her up like a doll. A flicker of anger starts to kindle. The grin on the bartender's face as he sees Kierian doesn't make him feel any better.

"Olgber! Set her down. Gently." Kierian waits until Cassie is fully on the ground before glaring at the troll. Olgber smiles smugly in return, baring the gaps of missing teeth. Kierian keeps what he wants to say to himself.

"Causing mischief as always," Kierian mutters. He's not sure if the troll hears him or not, but as glass slides down the bar to a customer, the sounds of the room begin to rise as normal. Their commotion can slip into the past and be forgotten. That's his hope, at least.

Kierian notes that Cassie, to her credit, has remained absolutely still. Her gaze is down, the palm of one hand set against her stomach. If they had time, he'd wait for her to say something first. The confusion and the weight of the world revealing itself is still too raw for him to revisit, even as he's watching her step through those same moments of realization. The buzz of the bar, specifically the hungry eyes of faces he recognizes, tells him they don't have the luxury of time.

Kierian closes the distance between them, turning his back on the room to try and shield her. Cassie meets his eyes, finally. "Are you okay?" he says.

"It doesn't take me to her," she says. She stares at him as she says it, frowning slightly as if he might change. "Why does it take me to you?"

Kierian doesn't have to work hard to put the pieces together. She's looking for her sister, but the imprint took her to him instead. "I can tell you," Kierian says. "But we can't stay here."

"Where would you go?"

Anywhere but here is his real answer, but he's not confident that's an answer that will convince her. "Out of the sight of the people..."

"People?" Cassie says, interrupting him.

"Out of the sight of the ones watching you," Kierian says. "I don't want them staring at us any more than you do." He can't speak freely enough to tell her why. He needs to get her away from here first.

Cassie is quiet, offering no further response. Kierian reaches one hand toward her. It's a small motion, not overly visible or attention drawing, but her eyes dart to his hand then back to his face.

"Will you come with me?" Kierian says. "That's the only way I can help you."

She studies him for a long moment before answering. "I don't trust you," she says. Her voice is barely audible above the noise.

Kierian nods. "I can't say I blame you," he says. He's not the biggest fan of himself at the moment either. "But please. Let me help you."

Cassie takes his hand. "Thank you," Kierian says. Without wasting any more time, Kierian leads her out of the bar. They can't go too far. Night will come quickly, and the streets aren't the place to get caught unaware. But he's been running. From the looks of it, she's been running too, trying to find him. He at least owes her an explanation of what is going on.

As soon as they're out of sight of the bar, Cassie's pace slows, and her hand drops from his. "Where are we going?" Cassie says. "And what happened?"

Both reasonable questions, ones that Kierian has not prepared for. He fumbles with his words, trying to figure out where to begin. "I'm trying to put a bit of distance between us and that place," Kierian says.

It's the best answer he can come up with. "You remember the other man in the shop? I don't trust him, and I want to get you away from him so he can't do anything to hurt you."

"You speak so highly of me, Kierian. I wonder what I ever did to deserve that honor." Kierian stiffens. He knows that voice.

"There's too many reasons to count, Pryor," Kierian says. "I don't think we need to relive all of them right now. Even you don't have that kind of time."

Kierian moves slowly, positioning himself between Cassie and Pryor. How the other vampire followed them Kierian isn't quite sure. How isn't the problem right now, though. Pryor isn't looking at him. He's looking at Cassie.

The grin on Pryor's face shows his bared teeth, a brushed aside red tint along his cheek. His sleeves aren't rolled up anymore. The blood there is fresh. Someone must have alerted him when Kierian came into the bar.

"What did I tell you?" Pryor says. "There's no point in wasting time. Once you know what it's like, there's no looking back."

"All that blood, and for what?" Kierian says. He takes stock of their surroundings. Cassie is still behind him. As far as he can tell, Pryor is alone. "A chance to add just a few more years to your life? I can't imagine yours is worth that much, or more than the one you're taking from."

Pryor laughs, the sound echoing off the alley walls. "Add enough years and who knows. All it takes is for you to get over yourself and realize what you've become."

"Did you ever stop to think maybe I never wanted this?" Kierian says. "Our court might have claimed me, made me when they put that disease in my blood, but it doesn't have to control me. I don't have to become what they want me to, what you think I should be."

Pryor takes a step forward. Kierian holds his ground. "What harm can it do?" Pryor says. "You've already been changed. What do you have left to lose?

"I don't think it matters what I say. There's nothing that can convince either of us to change our minds, is there?"

Pryor shrugs. "You know the consequences of not carrying this through," he says. "They wouldn't need much more than my word to call you to council."

"Then call a council meeting," Kierian says. "If they care enough to do something about me, let them cast their own judgement. Yours doesn't carry any weight."

Pryor bears his fangs. "You can't escape what you are. You can run from it, you can pretend all you want, but it's in your blood now."

"That doesn't mean I have to accept it outright," Kierian says. "We'll be going now. Come back with more force if you want to see things done your way."

It's a threat Kierian regrets the moment he speaks it. Pryor might do exactly that. But if that's what it comes to, Kierian can face it later. Kierian turns back to Cassie, gently placing a hand on her shoulder to direct her down the street. There're no footsteps behind them. Kierian doesn't look back, despite the urge to make sure Pryor isn't following them. That moment of weakness would only give Pryor more enjoyment. Kierian won't be the one to give him any pleasure of any kind, not if he has a say in it.

***

It's getting dark. There are fewer people on the street now, and Kierian isn't quite sure how long it's been since their run in with Pryor. They need to get somewhere safe or keep moving. In the absence of ideas for safe places, Kierian for a plan. Pulling one together while trying to figure out where to take them isn't an easy task.

Without any notice, Cassie pulls away from him. She stops, studying his face. Kierian slows down, stopping to one side of the sidewalk. "You said you were going to help me," Cassie says. "You still haven't told me where we're going or what's going on." He knew she would have questions, but he's still unprepared to answer them. His plan still isn't fully formed.

"I'm sorry," Kierian says. "I don't really have a place in mind yet. If we're not being followed, then things are going well. Which, we're not being followed. I've been looking out for us. Listen, I.... I know what it's like to imprint on someone, but I've never been on this side of it. I didn't want this to happen to you or anyone else."

Cassie frowns. "What do you mean?"

Knowing where to begin, or what specifically would be helpful for her to know, would make things easier. In the silence between his words, he watches her lean back against the brick exterior of a tall building. Her eyes narrow at him. Does she really want to know everything? He didn't. He still doesn't, but what else can he give her but the truth?

"Everything looks different, right?" Kierian asks. This time he keeps his focus, starting with the big picture then explaining the details. Cassie nods. When she doesn't say anything, he continues.

"You were never meant to see any of it," Kierian says. "Everything you're seeing is real. I'm real, I can promise you that much. This is what I really look like, and what the rest of the world looks like too without anything to shield you. You saw me change. I didn't realize it until later, but I dropped my guard trying to get Pryor to leave you alone. I was the first one you saw do that, the first one you saw as I really am. We call that imprinting."

"First one of what?" Her expression is neutral. He thinks she's absorbing the words he's saying but it's impossible to tell.

"Mythics," Kierian says. "That's what we call ourselves collectively. Those of us that aren't human, or at least not wholly." The ease of the explanation unsettles him. There's no hesitation to his words as he explains this. The reality of it has seeped into him. His acceptance of it isn't something he takes joy in.

Cassie blinks back at him. "I thought it would take me to my sister," she says. "Why did it take me to you?"

"That's how the imprint works," Kierian says. "I'm the reason you can see this world, so I'm supposed to be your guide of sorts. I connected you to it, so we're connected."

"I want to find my sister," Cassie says. "I don't know what all this is, but that's the one thing I want. Can you help me find her? Everything else... I don't know what else to think."

"What can you tell me about her?" Kierian says.

"She just disappeared last night," Cassie says. Her voice starts slow and even, but by the time she finishes her words run together. "Something happened to her and the first place I thought she'd go was that shop. She's always there. She brings back little overpriced trinkets, lining them up on her windowsill. Now they're broken on the floor. They got knocked over when the window was shattered. I can't find her. I feel like she'll be haunting the place if I go home. She was there last night and this morning she was gone and I..."

As she speaks, he can feel the bond waver. It's her. It couldn't be anything else, but seeing her right in front of him is both unnerving and a point of guilt. There's no running from this anymore. The point of guilt is only driven deeper by a suspicion that if her sister frequented the shop, Pryor would have seen her. Pryor, with his bloodied sleeves and secrets.

Kierian's scattered plan starts to take shape in his mind. He's still not quite convinced it will work, but it's the only thing he can think of. If Pryor did take her sister, or had any connection to it, then there's a chance Kierian knows where she's at. But to take Cassie into the heart of his clan's lair right now, he's almost certain it would end with blood. He wouldn't be able to live with himself if it were hers.

"I think I have a way to find your sister and get to her, but I need you to trust me," Kierian says. He almost regrets the words as her whole face brightens.

"You know where she is?" Cassie says. There's hope in her eyes but her voice tells him she can't quite believe it.

Kierian shakes his head. "I don't know for sure," he says. "But in order for us to have any chance at finding her, we have to do one thing first."

Cassie backs up one step, her eyes never leaving his face. She tilts her head slightly. "Not what Pryor wanted you to do?" she says.

"No," Kierian says. "Not that." He already made a promise to himself he would never turn anyone. He has no hesitation in promising her that. The court may be coming for him next, but not if he can make the source of their complaints disappear. They want him to bring her into the clan because she imprinted on him. There might be a way to undo it. He's never seen it done himself, but he's heard rumors. If their bond can be broken, Kierian can try and find her sister and Cassie might be able to return to her life again too.

"I can find you if something happens, can't I?" Cassie says. She breaks the quiet that's settled between them. Pressure starts to build against Kierian's ribs, but he lets it go.

"If I don't find you first," Kierian says. There's no way for him to know how this will end. His own life is shattered, still in pieces he's not sure how to recover. But if there's hope for Cassie, her sister, that's more purpose for his life than he's had in a while.

"There's a store across town that will have supplies," Kierian says. "But we need to get there before nightfall. Can you keep going?"

Cassie nods. "I'll follow you."

Chapter 4

Rounding a busy corner, Cassie ducks behind Kierian. She holds onto him tightly. They might be able to find each other but she'd like to not test that right now. With his attention focused ahead, she can't help but study him. He looks human from the side. His skin is still pale and cold to the touch. If he used to be human, that would make sense. But as she catches his eyes, there's that subtle reminder he's something else.

"We're almost there," Kierian says. The streets all seem to blur together. All Cassie is aware of is her feet hurting and her body starting to ache.

"Kier..." The moment she starts to say his name he stops abruptly. Every muscle in her body tightens, ready to run. He doesn't make any quick movements. Instead, he pulls her gently to the side of the street, setting them just inside the mouth of an alley.

"I didn't mean to scare you," he says. "But from here on it has to be half-names. That's the best way to protect both of us. You have to call me Kier."

She nods. "And I'm..."

"Cass."

She wrinkles her nose. "I've never liked Cass."

"Trust me, I don't like Kier either," he says. "But we're entering fae territory. There're only two things I need you to do. Let me lead, and don't stare."

"Fae?" Cassie says, her voice tentative.

"You'll know when you see them," Kierian says. He doesn't offer any additional explanation.

Cassie nods. She can't find much reason to argue with either of those points. Still, there's one unrelated question on her mind. "How do you know if a wall is or isn't really there?" Cassie says. "Like with the bar."

Kierian smiles. It's small, but Cassie still sees it. "I'm assuming you didn't figure that one out on your own?"

"I would have," Cassie says. "If I hadn't gotten pulled through first."

"It was built by mythic hands," Kierian says. "It's more of a curtain than a wall, really. The transparent look to it is what gives it away, at least for me. That's about as well as anyone else has explained it to me. Humans weren't the only ones who developed this city. It's older than most would probably believe."

There are more questions on Cassie's mind, but the change in surroundings draws her attention. Kierian leads her under a large arch, built into the stone buildings on either side of the road. Other than its size and age, there's nothing immediately distinct about it. Every different part of town has always had its character quirks. But as she passes underneath it, the air seems to change. It's different than it was moments ago, like they've crossed over into something new.

Edging from windows, underneath doorframes, and in the cracks of the brick and stone themselves, there's a dim, iridescent glow. The street itself exudes a warm haze. And it's not just the stone. Almost everyone around her is identified by a different warm tone. Each individual has a different shade to their veins, faint patterns on their skin, and the tint of their eyes. Colored veins seem to frame their eyes. Their faces are long and shallow. She can trace the bones underneath the surface of their skin, even more prominent than Kierian's. Only they're not quite where she'd expect those lines to be. Plates of bones, and even just the contours of their faces, aren't in the right place to be human. And their eyes are the same size, but they look like a dragonfly's. The surface of their wide eyes appear to be broken into multiple pieces, like fragments of a broken mirror. She almost forgets not to stare as they pass by.

Despite the strange sensation of this place, there's still something distinctly stunning about it. "It's beautiful," Cassie says. She speaks just loud enough for Kierian to hear her.

"It's supposed to be," he says. "There wouldn't be any temptation to give up everything and hide away here if it wasn't beautiful."

"I can't believe I would never have seen this otherwise," Cassie says. She can't help but feel a sense of wonder as she takes it all in. Seeing everything for the first time is an experience she can hardly put to words. But to know there's still more she can't see, more she doesn't know, lets fear undercut her wonder. She's no longer sure what she can trust.

***

They've passed over the border of his clan's territory, through the neutral fray of the city, and onto seelie ground. Kierian only glances over at Cassie when he has to. Every time he does, a vision flickers across his vision, changing her face: slitted eyes brown eyes, pale skin, her cheekbones more prominent, and something even more lost in her gaze. It's his imagination. She's as human as she ever was walking beside him. And yet, that's what they would have him do to her. Turn her. Let whatever it is that's run his course through him take root in her, change her, until she becomes one of them too.

Safety, though, holds fast at the front of Kierian's thoughts. There's nothing stopping them from harassing him, or going after her, until they get the ending they want. If the seelie can break their imprint, his clan has no more reason to go after either of them. The last thing they'll expect is for them to rush back in and find Cassie's sister. But every risk associated with his plan starts with the seelie being willing to help.

Every time the crowd jostles them, each time her hand tugs lightly at him, their bond ripples. Nothing is wrong, but he can't ignore the instinct that something might be. He can't save himself through her. He might not even be able to save her, much less her sister. But no matter how strong the urge to run away from it all, he stays rooted by her side.

Finally, Kierian spots what he's looking for. An apothecary. They should be able to point him toward whoever can help. Pressure builds in Kierian's chest. He lets it grow, expand, and slowly dissipate as he approaches the wooden doors. Nerves. His best-case scenario would be the two of them walking out having lost nothing but their imprint. His thoughts edge back from the worst case. Anything he might be able to imagine, he's positive could somehow end worse.

Kierian pauses at the foot of the steps leading up to the storefront. He can't look at her. The vision of her turned, he's not sure if that would propel him into or away from this place. "I know you might not trust me yet," he says. "But I need you to try. This is the best way I can think of to help us be able to find your sister."

"I want to trust you," Cassie says.

It's not the words he expected. She catches him off guard enough he lets himself look over, meeting her eyes. He's not sure what it is, but if she's willing to try and trust him he has to earn it. He hasn't done too well so far.

"Stay close." They're the only words he can think of saying before he takes the three steps up to the front doors of the apothecary. Curved semicircles in the wooden door emphasize the worn spots on the wood where hundreds, if not thousands, of hands have pushed their way through before them. Kierian opens it with his free hand, stepping through first. Cassie slips in behind him. Immediately a wave of spices hits his nose. The door shuts, sealing them in with the pungent scent.

Short, spinning racks take up most of the floor space, creating a walkway around the room and up to the counter. Open shelves of clear jars line the walls floor to ceiling. Kierian doesn't recognize the contents of most of the jars, but he's not particularly trying. Even if he wanted to read the script carved into the shelves to identify the contents, it's a language he can't read. The fae, seelie and unseelie, go back further in time than his own cursed kin.

A fae stands up behind the counter. Her hair falls over her shoulder in a thick, dark braid. Peach colored veins frame her face like rippling water. The same warm pink tints the bone-like plates on both sides of her jaw and her forearms. She leans forward, making eye contact with

Kierian first, then glances at Cassie. "Can I help you?" the fae says. "Most visitors don't wander in here on accident."

"We're not here on accident," Kierian says. "I was hoping you might be able to help us."

Kierian approaches the counter, weaving carefully between the short aisles. He's not quite sure if touching equates to buying here, but he'd rather not brush up against anything with unknown purposes or cost. Cassie follows close behind him.

"I can only help you if you tell me what you need," the fae says. "Otherwise, nothing will change."

Kierian knows what change he needs. He's practiced the words in his head. Every reason why has an answer to. He's tried hard not to think about what it might cost him, but he's not sure there's anything he wouldn't give if it let him try and save two lives.

"What can you tell me about imprints?" Kierian says. Cassie grips his hand tighter, but he doesn't dare break eye contact with the seelie fae.

The fae smiles, the sharpened points of her teeth revealing themselves. Her tone is as sweet and words as simple as if explaining something to a child. "They can only be broken two ways," she says. "Death of either party, which is the most common, or for the human to be changed. I suppose it wouldn't really matter whether it was you, someone, or something else that turned her. The result would be the same. That's not your real question, though, is it?"

"No," Kierian says. "There are rumors, ones I can't verify, saying your kind know of another way imprints can be broken. I want to know if that's true."

The fae's smile fades, hard lines returning to her face. He's not exactly sure how she does that. Moments after, he can feel Cassie pulling away from him, a sharp jolt carried along their bond. She almost pulls her hand from his.

"Cass," he starts, turning toward her.

She freezes when he looks at her, wide eyed and lips slightly parted.

"Cass?" he tries again.

"That's what you brought me here for?" she says. Her words start out as a whisper, her voice rising as her thoughts come tumbling out. "You told me you had a plan. You asked me if you could help, and I said yes. I told you what I could. You asked me to trust you and I wanted to. Everything isn't what it's supposed to be, but I still wanted to try. But she's not here, is she? Whatever you plan is..."

"I can't help her if they won't stop hunting us until you're turned. I had to protect you first, then..."

The fae interrupts them both, her words cutting through the air like ice. Even the silence seems frozen in her wake. "Even if that were something I could do, both of you would need to be in agreement. That is clearly not the case here. An imprint runs deeply through both human and mystic. It would be impossible to dissolve it through unwanted external interference. There's a reason some things stay as rumors."

Kierian glances over his shoulder at the fae. Her arms are crossed as she leans against the wall behind her. She's not looking at him, though. She's not looking at either of them. Kierian follows her gaze to the door they came in and out onto the street. Something isn't right. If she's waiting for something...

Kierian gently takes hold of Cassie's shoulders, drawing her attention. "We need to go," he says. His voice is low and quiet. It probably wouldn't matter if anyone else heard him, but he would rather not take any more chances. He probably already made too many mistakes. If this fae won't help him, there's nothing else for them here.

"Why?" Cassie says. "Why would I..."

"I'm sorry," Kierian says, the words cutting through him. "But something isn't right here. We need to go now. Will you follow me? We're not staying here. I can promise you that."

Cassie nods once.

"Thank you." Still just as careful not to touch anything, Kierian heads for the door. Cassie stays close behind him. He doesn't look back. Instead, he keeps his gaze set ahead as empty streets stare back at him.

Chapter 5

No matter what streets they go down, Kierian can't spot a single fae. The darkened windows are eerie. Kierian can feel stares from behind the glass, but it doesn't matter. If they can't get beyond this sector's limits before something catches up to them, he's not sure what will happen. He hasn't spent any time in the seelie court, but from the stories he's heard, he'd rather not start now.

As Kierian ducks down another street, footsteps echo behind them. He glances back but there's still no one visible. Beside them, sounds ricochet. Kierian doesn't change his path. If he's headed the correct way, they're almost there. If they can hold their ground a little longer...

Kierian turns a corner onto the main street and slams to a halt. Cassie runs into him, and he stops moments before colliding with the seelie guard. Their dark, compound eyes stare at him. Sun crests are embroidered just above their hearts, at least where Kierian would assume their hearts to be. Arms exposed with light pink veins, from their wrists up through their forearms, with small ivory spikes protruding. He's never thought too much about it. Now he's wondering how sharp they are.

He's half convinced he could make it if he ran, but that would mean leaving Cassie behind. He got her into this mess. He's going to be the one to fix it. That might be more than his two hands can do, but that won't stop him from trying.

A voice calls out. Kierian can't see who it belongs to through the sea of fae. "Sieze them, please."

Immediately the guards reach for them. Kierian jerks back but they catch his shoulder as he turns. His arms are twisted sharply behind his back. He grimaces, forcing back his fangs. Cassie gasps. As far as he can tell, she's still okay.

A small gap in the guards' rank forms. A tall seelie fae strides toward them. He doesn't break eye contact with Kierian as he walks. His hands are behind his back as well, only his are held by his own will. He has a golden color running through his veins, creating a pattern on the fae's face like an intricately painted mask. He pauses a few feet away from Kierian, tilting his head and smiling to reveal sharp teeth.

"I heard you might be coming here," the fae says. "What I wasn't expecting was your request. Seeking answers to rumors in fae territory is a dangerous ordeal, especially at night. Asking questions about imprints... That's bravely foolish. However, that line of questioning, including its intentions and your sources, is one we cannot let go uninspected. You will both be called to our court. It is there you can present your case for your presence and purpose here. Until then, you will wait."

Kierian narrows his eyes at the fae, keeping his feet firmly in place. "Why would you have to take action if your kind refused? No wrong was done on either side."

"You put your trust in an unknown," says the fae. "That's something not everyone can do, so you have my respect in that. But imprints are much more than something to be made and broken at will. As such, we cannot have word spreading that we can or cannot break them. There are already some mythics who see no consequence or responsibility to being a part of a bond. To confirm or deny would only increase the number of those who believe that. So, we must always deny the request, as we have never tested to determine if it's possible or not."

"And what if I were to object, on behalf of the court of my own clan?" Kierian says. The words come out before he can fully think them through, but he does his best to look like he's serious.

The fae leans forward. "You don't know who I am, do you?" he says. "I am the prince over this court. Right or wrong, you will see justice here before finding out what judgement yours will deliver."

"Whatever my court has told you..." Kierian starts to speak, but the prince raises a hand to silence him.

"We will hold you here until a decision in the court can be made," the prince says.

"Please, you have to understand..." Cassie starts to speak, but her voice is drowned out.

"We will hear your pleas after, if you wish," the prince says. "But that time has not yet come. Fall in."

As the prince moves to the front of the procession, the guards close rank behind him. Without any further instructions, the fae holding them start to move down the street. Kierian is pulled forward. He loses sight of Cassie. He twists sharply but is held in place.

"Cass!"

"Kier!"

Kierian can feel Cassie struggling, pushing toward him. It takes all his strength to stay steady and not fight back. If there's any chance it might help them stay together and not get separated, he will keep himself together no matter what he feels under the surface.

***

Cassie's heart drops, the shadow of a large building looming over them as they approach it. A relatively intact fire escape scales the building, a few figures standing on the outdoor landings. The windows are blacked out with bars over every other one. They stop in front of the main doors. The guards part, creating a pathway to the front door. It's already open. Kierian, restrained by guards, passes just ahead of her through the wall of fae. She's led just behind him.

The prince stands to one side just inside the door. Cassie can feel him watching her, but she stares at Kierian's back. It takes all her strength to suppress the panic rising in her. She's not sure how much more she can take. Off to the side of the foyer, a door is opened revealing a narrow staircase. Kierian is pushed toward it, the hands on Cassie's arms tightening. A new voice cuts through the shuffling of feet, and the guards pause.

"Let me take them. They've caused enough disturbance today. They don't have anywhere to run. They wouldn't get very far if they tried." It's a feminine voice, one that echoes from behind them.

"Are you sure this isn't a job that's below you?" the prince says.

"Isn't this job below you? I believe you have more important things to do. Let your right-hand handle this."

The silence is thick. Cassie can feel the weight of the guards shifting. Kierian stares straight ahead, his hands curling into fists then relaxing. There's a low hum to their bond she can't interpret.

There are no further words spoken, but the hands holding Cassie release her. They let Kierian go as well. He turns slowly toward her. He makes eye contact for just a moment before looking past her. Cassie turns around to find hazel eyes, a faint pattern from the fae's neck down her arms in a matching hue until the veins disappear beneath a set of light purple gloves.

"I'm Flora," the fae says. There's a cheeriness to her voice that doesn't seem to match the smile on her face. They both feel forced. "If you go peacefully, you only have to deal with me. Otherwise, it's a lot less enjoyable for you." She doesn't end with a question, but Cassie can hear it in the silence. Will they accept those terms?

"Where are we going?" Kierian says. Cassie stands very still, waiting.

"Up the stairs, fourth landing," Flora says. "I'll be right behind you."

Kierian pauses, then meets Cassie's gaze again. Cassie steps toward him. No one stops her. No one says anything at all. She keeps going until she's standing next to him, then another few steps toward the stairs. Kierian stays by her side. A few whispers rise up behind them but the door to the stairwell closes before Cassie can decipher them.

Cassie counts each landing as they go until they reach the fourth one. She hesitates, waiting for Flora's instructions. "This one. Go through that door and take a left."

Kierian opens the door, holding it while she passes through. Just two doors down, Flora speaks again. "Hold here."

Cassie pauses. Flora approaches and pulls out a ring of keys. When she turns her attention to Cassie and Kierian, there's something different about her. The seriousness of her features isn't forced.

"I need the two of you to move slowly and stay calm," Flora says. Her voice is low and even, but her gaze doesn't move from Kierian. "Why did you want to break your imprint?"

Kierian's eye twitches. "Do you really want to know?"

Flora puts the key in the lock without looking away. It clicks. "I'm listening."

Kierian clenches his jaw. "My clan has a different idea of how imprints should be handled than I do," he says. The words are direct and to the point. "If our imprint was broken, they wouldn't have a reason to hunt either of us. That's what I wanted."

"What're you doing with an imprint then, if you don't want to turn her?" Flora says.

Kierian doesn't answer. The silence stretches, the tension pliable. Flora turns the key in the lock. It clicks again and she pushes it open. The door squeals on its hinges, revealing a room with only wood floors, a woven rug, and dark fabric hung over the far window. Deep scratches mar the wood along the walls. Cassie shivers.

"I was trying to protect her," Kierian says, his voice low as if forcing the words out. "I didn't do this on purpose, but I couldn't stand by and let something happen to her when I thought she was in danger, even if she was a stranger."

"And?" Flora says.

"And I'd rather help her than leave her to fend for herself. Are we done here, or do you want something?" Kierian says.

Flora smiles. Wide and bug-like, Flora's expression is nearly impossible to read. "If you want to face the seelie court you're welcome to. I won't stand in your way or theirs. If you'd like a chance to avoid that fate, I need the two of you to trust me."

Kierian narrows his eyes, the slits of his pupils becoming more prominent. "It sounds like a trap either way."

Flora spins the key on one finger, breaking eye contact with Kierian to watch it. "Maybe," she says. "What I can confidently say is on one hand, you have a fae prince who relies on his own definition of justice. On the other, you have a fae who knows what it's like to care about the fate of her imprint."

"Where are they?" Cassie asks. Kierian grips her hand tighter, but Cassie continues. "If you cared about them, why aren't they here?"

Flora flicks the key around a bony finger, and it twirls once before she catches it in the palm of her hand. "You know what they'd do to you if they caught you," she says to Cassie. There's a tangible weight to her words. "I didn't think they could catch him, but they did. So, you could say I have a different idea of the value of an imprint than my court does."

"You still haven't told us what you want from us," Kierian says.

Flora is quiet for a moment, rubbing the head of the key with her thumb. "I can't stay here," she says finally. "I almost left a long time ago, but without a clean break they can always take me back. The prince thinks my role is one of honor, but he also won't let me go. Others have slipped away but he would notice me.

"So, I need your help." Flora tilts her head to one side, the motion just a little too far that it's slightly unsettling. "You're both as much strangers to me as I am to you. I want to break you out. Then I'm leaving on your terms, not my own. If I don't leave for myself they can't drag me back, at least not as easily."

Before either of them can respond, Flora turns sharply, glancing back down the hallway. Cassie can't hear anything unusual, but that doesn't mean they're alone. Flora turns back to them with the key in her hand, the gold standing out against the purple glove.

"Wait for me in there," Flora says. "I'll be back. If I'm not, then none of it matters, does it?"

Kierian starts to speak, but Flora cuts him off. "Now. Before someone else decides words aren't persuasive enough."

Kierian stands for a moment longer in the hallway. He reaches for the key and Flora doesn't stop him. As soon as it's in his hands, Flora sprints down the hallway back the way they came, her footsteps soft. Cassie glances down the hall, waiting until Flora disappears through the door they came in and down the steps.

Chapter 6

Kierian steps into the dim room. The curtains at the far end flutter. Cassie steps inside after him. Kierian shuts the door behind her but leaves it unlocked. He still holds the key in his hands.

There are too many unknowns. He holds the key to this room but it's worth so little. They could try and escape, but the cost of getting caught again is more than he's willing to risk. Flora might be coming back. She knows more about them than he'd like, and they know precious little about her. She has a plan, but her motivations are a mystery. Getting wrapped up in a fae plot is the last thing he wants to get involved in.

The surest course of action is to wait for the Seelie court, receive their verdict, and live through the sentence. That's the only outcome Kierian can think of concretely. But then they would lose every chance of finding Cassie's sister before it's too late.

"What are we supposed to do?" Cassie says. Her voice hardly makes a dent in the space. She stands in the center of the room, arms crossed over her chest as she stares at him. There's no tension in their imprint. If anything, it's as if there's more space between them than physically possible.

"We have to wait," Kierian says. He falls silent, the rest of his thoughts refusing to form cohesive sentences.

Cassie continues to watch him. Her eyes seem to scan his face. It makes it hard to look at her when he doesn't know what she's thinking, when he can imagine more than a few accusatory statements aimed at himself.

"What if she comes back?" Cassie says.

Kierian shakes his head. "Whatever she wants, we can't trust her."

"Why?" Cassie says. She takes a deep breath, her cheeks flushing as she continues. "Why not? I don't know if anyone is chasing us. If you're telling me the truth, I think I know what your clan wants with me. All I want is to find my sister. Can you really help me find her, or did you just need me to come with you for your own sake?"

The words cut Kierian deeply, caught off guard by the force of her words and the unmoving stare leveled at him. Their bond hums, though he's not quite sure which one of them it's moving in response to.

"I thought if I could give my clan a reason to stop following us we'd be free to find your sister," Kierian says. "I promised myself from the start I wouldn't hurt you. That's why we're here. I thought the fae could break our bond. That would keep my clan hunting you, then we could rescue your sister. I never thought this would happen. I'm still trying to figure out the best way to get out of here."

A beat passes before Cassie speaks again. "Do you know where my sister is?" The question is fragile, as if it could break in the distance between the two of them.

Pryor's face and the back room in the antique store, like scenes from another lifetime, flash in his mind. The blood on the back door. The blood on Pryor's clothes. He should have known better even before Cassie stepped foot into that store. He promised himself he wouldn't take part, but he didn't do anything about what might have been happening just one room away.

Kierian's answer sounds hollow, even to his own ears. "I think so. I won't know for sure until we get there, but..."

"Get where?" The intensity of her attention contrasts sharply with her softly spoken words. It drives a knife into Kierian's chest, one he put there himself.

"She's not the only one who has disappeared near that antique store," he says. Cassie takes a step away from him, but he keeps going. "We have to go back to my clan. If they're the ones that took her, which I think they are, that's where she'll be. There's no one else, at least not a mythic, who would take her off those streets near there. That's my clan's territory."

Cassie sucks in a sharp breath. Kierian holds his ground, trying to let her be in control of the room. He stands still. She backs up toward the wall opposite him.

"I didn't know how else to try and save her if it meant putting you both at risk of the same fate," Kierian says. "This was the only plan I could think of that might save both of you."

Maybe he was wrong. Maybe there was something else he could have done. They could have made a million different choices had anything gone differently. But even as she stares back at him with her arms crossed over her chest, he knows her heart is still beating. The air in her lungs is serving its purpose and the blood running through her veins is enough to sustain her. Keeping her alive, truly alive, is worth taking risks. He can only hope it's enough in the end, whatever that end may be.

"I was so close." Cassie sways, her eyes on the ground. "I was so close to finding her and I didn't know?"

"I won't know for sure until we find her," Kierian says. For all his suspicions, for all his efforts, it might be for nothing. It still might be too late. "If they took her, though, that's where she'd be now. You don't have to trust me, just don't give up, okay? I might've gotten us into this mess, but I want to help you find her and keep you safe. Just don't give up."

Cassie stares back at him. Their imprint thrums like the echo of her heartbeat, but he can't read her mind. He can't tell what she's thinking, though he wishes he could. But he's made his choice, every choice that's led up to standing in this barren room covered in what he has to believe is dust. Wherever he's fallen on the scale of right and wrong, they're here now. He wants to help her, but she has to let him.

"What happens if she isn't there?" Cassie leans back against the far wall, arms still crossed firmly over her chest. She's holding on so tightly to herself Kierian can't help but wonder if it hurts.

"Then we keep looking," Kierian says. "For however long it takes, for as long as you'll let me search with you. We will keep going until we find her."

She presses her lips together, her eyes moving across his face. "I don't know if you're telling the truth," she says. "I don't trust you. Not after you asked, not after we ended up here. I wanted to, but not anymore."

"Again, I can't fault you for that," Kierian says. "But it doesn't mean I'm not telling the truth."

"Why?" Cassie says. "You've never hesitated. You don't even know my sister but you keep saying you haven't done anything but try and help me. Why bother trying to save her if she's a stranger and I'm hardly more than that?"

"Because I'd have given anything for someone, anyone, to rescue me out of that place before it was too late."

His words tear open a wound in his heart, one deep and one he thought had died along with so many other pieces of his life. Pain echoes through him, very much alive. The memories themselves aren't clear. They're hardly more than hazy shapes that populate his nightmares, but he knows what happened to him. He was changed, not by his own will, and there's something that's taken root in him because of it.

"If I can save even one soul from that," Kierian says. "I would do anything. I was too afraid to keep that promise before, but I'm not anymore."

The truth feels settled outside himself. It's not pleasant. There's no way to know what might have changed if he'd done any number of things differently. But he's left with Cassie staring across the dim room at him, waiting for her reply.

"I believe you."

It's all she says. Those three words can't heal a wound that feels like a life's burden, but the reception of the words releases a weight on him that brings to his knees. He bends his head toward the ground, not quite brave enough to look up at her, not quite confident in his strength to stand.

"I've never said any of that out loud," Kierian says. The words are mostly for himself, but he can hear the faint rustling of her movements. He closes his eyes as he feels a hand on his shoulder, a momentary shock running through him as it pulls back, then rests on him again.

"Thank you," Cassie says. "For trusting me with it."

The words are soft, not coming from above him. Kierian lifts his head and opens his eyes. Her hand falls from his shoulder but she remains crouched across from him. A thousand words cross his mind in those moments, but only one question comes out.

"Will you let me help you?" he says.

She pauses a moment before answering. "Will you tell me the whole truth? No more lies to try and protect me."

"I don't know what's ahead of us, but if I'm able, yes. The whole truth."

She reaches out a hand to him. It's not extended far, since she's not more than a foot from him, but she sets it there in front of him. "I will let you help me."

He takes her hand, pulling himself to his feet as she stands up too. His lips part, words on his tongue. They both jump when the door to the room creaks open. A face peers around it, staring at them. From just the bug eyes alone it's hard to tell who they belong to, but it's the hazel tint of veins beneath the plates of skin that clue him in. It's not until she speaks that he's confident who the fae is.

"Am I interrupting something?" Flora says. She doesn't leave enough time for an answer. "If we're leaving, we're leaving now. This may be the only chance we get. Are you coming with me or not?"

Cassie rubs at her eyes, leaving them slightly red and puffy. Kierian's gut instinct is still to refuse. As he looks between the fae and Cassie, the answer that slips out is different.

"Yes. We're coming."

"Great," Flora says. "Now, if you'll follow..."

"We might need your help too," Cassie says. Kierian can hear the waver in her voice. But she keeps going despite it. "You help us first. We help you second. If you're telling us the rest of your plan later, we can tell you what we need later too."

Flora steps out of the doorway. She grins, looking first at Kierian. "She learns fast." Then, to Cassie, "You've got yourself a deal. Can I get your name?"

Kierian cuts in before Cassie can answer. "Can you get us out of here?"

Flora's smile never falters. "Follow me."

Chapter 7

FLORA LEADS THE WAY down the hall. There's a sharpness to her movements. Precise and methodical, there's no room for error. It's as if she's more aware of the space around her than Cassie could ever hope to be. Still, her brain tells her there's something not quite human about the fae, if she's even human at all.

Flora doesn't take them to the staircase they came up earlier. She pauses in front of iron bars that guard a lift much older than Cassie would like to imagine. Flora pulls opens the first layer of metal grating with gloved hands. The inner part folds to one side. Flora holds the iron back on one side, the tension holding both halves of the grate open. Cassie starts to speak, but Flora shakes her head, lifting one finger to her lips. Cassie's never really been afraid of elevators, heights, or small spaces, but this tests her.

Kierian steps in first. He tests the elevator floor, pressing on it with his foot. When it holds him, he steps fully onto it. He reaches out a hand and Cassie takes it. So far it holds both their weight. They leave enough space for Flora to come in, but she lingers. A door opens and shuts down the hall, footsteps echoing. Kierian leans forward but he doesn't touch the iron gates. Flora quickly closes the inner layers of the lift, then peels off her gloves. She tosses them through the grating and they disappear through a gap between the floor of the lift and the hallway. She turns her back on them, facing the noise.

"Flora." The manufactured sweetness to the prince's voice wraps around Cassie like a snake even though the words aren't meant for her. "Are you sure you know what you're doing? Don't do something you'll live to regret."

"All those years ago I didn't know what was at stake," Flora says. There's an edge to her words, despite her polite tone. "I thought I wanted this. I thought I knew exactly who you were, how this game of position and power was played. What would it cost me? More than I wanted to pay. Trust me. This time I know exactly what I'm doing."

The prince tilts his head slightly. "Then why now?" he says. "If it cost you so much, why wait? You could have done anything you wanted. It would have cost you then too, but you were free to make that choice. So why now?"

Flora tenses. "Maybe it took me this long to realize what you stole from me."

"You'd give this all up?" the prince says. "The place all young fae seek after when joining the court is the one you're in. Right hand to the prince of the seelie court, representative to the unseelie. Your voice is heard directly by the one who can act upon your advice. You know the place I rescued you from. You know the opportunity you sought out when I offered you a place in my court. This is where you belong. This is your home."

A shutter runs through Flora. "How could I forget?" Flora says, her teeth gritted. "I wasn't nothing before you took me under your wing, I was only less. Isn't that right? I was only of value once I was yours."

"Is this really how you want to fall?" the prince says. "You should know better than anyone what it looks like to cast my warnings aside."

Flora takes a deep breath. She crosses her arms over her stomach, her hands curling into fists. "That blood isn't on my hands."

One corner of the prince's lips curl up. "And it's on mine?" the prince says. "Oh Flora, you've lived long enough to know how this works. Don't tell me you've forgotten what you are. Who you were made to be. I thought I taught you better than this."

"It's their story now," Flora says. She takes a step back toward the elevator. The doors are still closed, Cassie and Kierian inside the stationary lift. "I know what my story has been up to this moment, but I'm not putting it in your hands any longer. I am taking back control."

She takes one more step back, just inches from the metal grating. Flora continues. "You want my gratitude? You want my thanks for what you made me to be when I didn't know what that would mean for my life? Here's my repayment."

Flora turns sharply toward the lift door. She only hesitates for a moment before her bare hands close around the grating to the lift, pulling it open. She cries out, the metal clipping her shoulder as she slips inside. Tears pool below her eyes, red skin on her hands and shoulder where she contacted the metal.

"We're leaving," Flora says. She punches a button on the lift with enough strength she hisses, recoiling her hand. "I am leaving, and once I cross the lines of this territory I am not coming back."

The lift shutters to life, a deep groan coming from its mechanical systems as it starts to move. The prince approaches the grate slowly. The lift lowers as the prince looks down on them through the grate. "I won't take that as a binding word," the prince says. "Not yet. Whether you make it past these bounds or not, the next time you see me my offer will be final."

Flora doesn't look up. Eyes closed, head bowed, and arms crossed over her chest, her voice comes out a whisper. "Good." The one word carries a bitterness that can only be grown by many years – of resentment, anger, or grief, Cassie isn't sure.

The lift shutters again when it hits the main floor. The iron rattles, a new grate in front of them now. A distant bell rings as if to signify their arrival. "If you'd be so kind as to unlock and open the doors..." Flora's voice trails off, but she looks right at Cassie.

"Cass," she answers. It's not quite as easy as the fae made it look to open it. grabs the door, pulling at it, but it only rattles in place. She frowns, partly out of concentration and partly frustration.

"Can I help?" Kierian says. Cassie nods without looking at him. Her focus is so narrowly on the iron grating, it's not until he puts his hands on top of hers that she realizes she didn't quite understand the help he was offering.

"Don't let go," Kierian says. "I can't pull this open on my own unless I end up like Flora over here."

Cassie focuses on his words and the cold iron beneath her fingers. She pulls as hard as she can. Kierian's hands grip hers, the palm of her hands digging deep into the grating. But with one final pull, it releases. When the sliding piece clicks into place, it stays open on its own.

The three of them quickly exit the lift. The main floor's hallway is dimly lit, only one emergency exit and a hard corner that likely would take them back to the front door. For the moment, they're alone.

"Wait here," Flora says. "If you see me come back around that corner you can come out. Otherwise, it's up to the two of you how far you get."

Those words don't fill Cassie with confidence as Flora walks away from them. Flora's footsteps echo down the hall, her voice carrying but slightly muffled.

"Guard! What are your orders?"

There's a faint rustling, then an answer. "Waiting for the return of the prince, lady."

"He is occupied at the moment, and he has stated that he will be for some time," Flora says. "He's asked me to carry orders for an inspection of the fire escapes to be carried out by the time he has finished."

"We take orders from the prince."

"I am his aid and he has instructed me to speak on his behalf. Will you listen to his word or neglect it simply because it comes from me? I know who you are, soldier."

There is no answer, at least not one that Cassie can hear. A few more moments pass in tense silence before Flora's head pops around the corner again. "As soon as we leave this building, we don't stop until we pass the edge of the seelie sector," she says. "Do you understand? You'll know when you've made it."

"We're ready," Kierian says. The confidence in his voice supports her. Cassie wishes she could feel it herself. Freezing up in this place, though, is something she'd like to avoid. She would rather take her chances with running than staying here any longer.

Flora slips around the corner. Kierian and Cassie follow, crossing the foyer after her. Flora tests the door, pushing it out slightly and letting it fall shut without incident. She opens it again and motions Kierian and Cassie through. As soon as it clicks shut behind them, Flora starts running. They make it down the street and around a corner before shouts go up behind them.

Flora guides them through small, narrow streets. They adjust their pace in more crowded areas. No matter what they do, the three of them draw attention. They gather stares and more than a few hushed remarks Cassie counts herself glad she can't hear. Cassie keeps her eyes on Flora, letting the imprint tell her how far Kierian is behind.

Flora stops abruptly at a street corner. Across a four-way intersection, the street ahead of them passes between two large stone buildings. The cobblestone transitions to the brick of the inner city. The boundary appears to be clear. Mythics pass in and out with no trouble, but just inside small windows, inset with no glass or barrier, a fae sits checking those who come and go.

Flora turns to Kierian with a frown. "There's not enough traffic to disguise us," she says. "We can try another section of the boundary, but I don't think it will matter. That will only give them more time to prepare to stop us."

"Do they know about us yet?" Kierian says.

Flora shrugs. "I'd have to assume so. I couldn't exactly make our exit a stealthy one. Word travels quickly when it needs to."

"Will they recognize us without you?" Kierian says. He tilts his head slightly at Cassie.

Flora studies her. "I don't think so," she says. "I think they'll be coming for me first. Catching the two of you would be a bonus for them. If you can get past them here, I'll find my own way out."

Kierian nods. "Then we'll meet you on the other side."

"I'll find you." Flora moves quickly away from them, turning down a side street and disappearing from view.

"If they're not looking for us then this is easy," Kierian says. "We just walk out."

Cassie nods, but when he doesn't continue, she prompts him. "What if they do recognize us?" she says. "What's the plan then?"

Kierian doesn't make eye contact with her when he answers. "I show them what I am," he says. "There are some mythic rules that have history longer than I know. By our imprint, if I lay claim to you, none of them can touch you."

Her questions pile up, threatening to tilt her world more sideways than it already is. "What does that mean?" she asks. She already has a pretty good idea, but she can't say yes without asking.

Kierian tenses, his gaze passing over her face. "I promised before and I'll promise again not to hurt you, but they don't know that. They can't know that. I need your answer before we do anything. If you say no, we can try and find a different way."

Cassie's heartbeat races. A coldness creeps over her. It threatens to keep her rooted in place. If she says nothing, nothing happens. She could say no, find another way to try and end this nightmare. But even if she squeezes her eyes shut, they'll still open to Kierian's deep slit eyes, two teeth just barely hidden by his bottom lip, and a whole world of other sights that refuse to disappear. Standing still only lets this world catch her in its grips.

"I'll follow your lead." Cassie reaches out her hand. Kierian takes it, hesitating only for a moment before striding quickly down the street toward the seelie boundary.

Chapter 8

KIERIAN KEEPS HIS FOCUS ahead as he leads Cassie down the main boulevard. Kierian walks between Cassie and the street, careful to keep her far away from walls and other mythics on the street as possible. All they have to do is pass between those buildings, get past the guards, and they're on their way. The seelie shouldn't follow them. Bureaucracy moves slower than that.

They approach the last bit of street, the shadow of the guard towers looming over them. Fae pass in and out. Kierian tries to keep them in the center of it all, but he can't disguise what they are. They're almost through when a sharp, piercing whistle cuts through the air. Kierian winces. Cassie glances over, a slight frown as he shakes his head. "They know who we are," Kierian says. There's no other explanation in his mind.

Before he can change his mind, he picks Cassie up, sweeping her feet off the ground. Kierian starts off slow, feeling the weight of her in his arms for a few paces. Once he's sure he won't drop her he starts to run. The mythics around him part like a river.

Two fae, one on either side of the street, appear from their respective buildings and onto the street. Kierian does not slow down.

"Hey, where are you going!"

The two guards jog toward the center of the street, eyes on Kierian. He makes eye contact with one of them. Kierian falters, a shutter running through his bones. His pupils dilate as his fangs elongate. He can feel them press into his bottom lip before he bares them. He's now acutely aware of every place his body touches Cassie. Right now, the heat of her is all he can focus on. He has to pull back soon, otherwise he might break his promise and he couldn't forgive himself for that. Every impact of his feet against the ground is a grain falling through an hourglass. If the last one runs through he's not sure what will happen.

Other than the bloodthirst with his fangs out, this is his least favorite thing. This is as close as he can get to seeing the fae in their whole forms. White antennae raise from the top of their heads, their mouths changing from lips to a much more insect-like maw. Like a praying mantis, only the same size as him.

The guards take a few steps to the side as a growl rises unbidden from the back of Kierian's throat. Their momentary stillness tells him all he needs. The ancient right works. Cassie's hands squeeze tighter around him as he bursts past the fae and across the line drawn somewhere deep within the earth below. All he has to do now is come back to himself.

He's not sure what street he's on or where he's going, but that's not Kierian's first worry. He picks a street to turn down and makes one more corner before he comes to a stop. Cassie is curled into a tight form in his arms. He sets her down gently but the tension in his body doesn't relax. Every nerve is on edge.

"Kierian?"

Her voice. Cassie's voice. She's standing now, hair wild as it frames her face. He keeps avoiding her eyes. There's a heat emanating from their bond that draws him toward her like a moth to a flame. Her heart beats faster. He can feel her pulse, even though he's not touching her. Kierian stumbles to one side, leaning heavily against the brick wall. He clenches his fists and digs his nails into his palms, willing the pain to distract him.

"Kier."

He frowns at the shortening of his name. He starts to reply, and in that motion remembers his state. His fangs are still out.

He focuses on his fangs. If he can get them to pull back, the rest of himself should follow. Cassie stays perfectly still, only her lungs and heart moving. He pictures her eyes, then her hair. The t-shirt she's wearing, down to her shoes. He imagines the image of her, but in a way that lets him remember that humanity in her he used to have - humanity he still wishes he could get back.

Finally, as a final push, he tries to picture the bottom of her shoes – something he's never paid close attention to before but staring at the ground they're just within his peripheral vision. They're probably covered in dirt, little rocks, and other pieces of junk wedged in the gaps. Those little things have to be separate from her, otherwise he'll just keep spiraling. He can't keep his promise if he reclaims himself once there's blood on his hands.

If Kierian still had the ability to gasp, he would. Pain explodes through his body. He stumbles backward, the force behind it like a punch to the gut. As he struggles to right himself, there's a relief that floods through him as his fangs retract. Every muscle in his body feels tired. Exhaustion threatens to pull him down to the ground. He can't rest yet, though.

"I'm okay," he says. His voice wavers, but he's able to push against the wall enough to stand up.

There's a visible tension in her body. "I'm okay," he says again, though he doesn't move from the wall. "I promise. How are you?"

It takes a moment for her to answer. "What was that?" she says. "I haven't seen you like that before. The imprint also felt... different."

He glances away from her, his features falling. "That's what a vampire going after blood looks like," Kierian says. His voice is low and even. "When I promised I'd never hurt you, that's what I mean. In any state, but especially that one."

"Do you need it?" she says.

"Blood?" Kierian hates asking the question. Cassie nods. A moment of silence passes before Kierian answers.

"No," he says. "Blood is how the disease is passed on. How it alters humans. The real purpose vampires take it is to chase after immortality. None of us can live forever, but some are determined to try. I don't need it. I don't want it. I've never wanted to try, and I don't particularly want to live forever."

Before he can keep talking and make a fool out of himself, one gunshot rings through the air. Both Cassie and Kierian jump. "I almost hope that was Flora," Kierian mutters.

***

Flora squeezes her eyes shut the moment she pulls the trigger. Sound seems to shatter the air around her as the pistol remains aimed through the open window. Her antenna twitch rapidly, the sound ringing in her head. Her grip on the pistol remains strong. Her arm wavers slightly, but the barrel remains pointed toward the top floor of an abandoned building, only its ground floor still in use.

The weapons bunker seems to have a warmth to it, like she's using it for the exact purpose it was built. For a moment, it's just Flora and every sort of weapon hanging from the walls. She didn't get to where she is now without learning how to use them, but there's no point in bringing all of them. All she needs is one. It won't take them long to find this bunker. It will take them even less time to figure out which direction she ran to escape.

"I'll be gone before you can catch me," Flora mutters. She holsters the pistol, concealing it beneath the folds of a long shawl tied at her waist.

She leaves the bunker behind, darting down a side street. She turns down two more before she steps out into the open again down the main street. Most of the streets are cleared. It's mostly guards running through the streets, running in every direction. Everyone else speaks in hushed whispers. As far as she can tell, Flora is the only one not going home.

Flora heads back down the street where she left the vampire and his imprint. That might be what they're expecting, but it's her best shot at finding the two of them again. Flora frowns as she walks up the street. There's one guard standing in the center of the road, arms crossed and scanning the crowd. Everyone breaks off before they reach him. If they belong in this sector, they have no reason to pass over into the inner city. She isn't staying here, though. She no longer belongs.

Flora continues down the street, meeting the guard's eyes as she approaches him. He locks eyes with her. Whether it's out of recognition or not, Flora can't tell. She sets one hand on the grip of the pistol, careful not to reveal it. The guard mirrors her movement. Flora clenches her jaw but keeps moving forward. No element of surprise. She'll draw, but only if he makes the first move. It's the guard who breaks the silence first.

"Flora?" He recognizes her, and she recognizes his voice.

"Ingram." She nods as she says his name. "Give my regards to the prince." His mouth is still slightly parted, antennae curled slightly.

"I can't let you..."

"Can't you?" Flora says. "He would want me alive, no bullet in me, and I don't want to shoot you. Don't make me."

The fae takes one step back. It's a formality more than permission. "Don't do something you'll regret," he says quietly.

Flora smiles grimly. "That's what he said too. It's far too late for that."

The fae watches her leave, one hand still on his weapon but he doesn't move to stop her. It's the one thing she'd thank the prince for, if she ever had to choose something. The position of power he gave her made everyone else too afraid to touch her, even as she leaves it all behind. As soon as she feels herself pass the territorial barrier, something lifts from her shoulders and she starts to run.

She takes the first street she can find, then the second one before she starts to slow down. There's no indication of where Cass and her mythic might have gone. Even as Flora scours the street for any signs, she passes her hand over different scuffs and debris briefly before moving on. The walls of the city give her no assistance either.

Flora wanders the streets, keeping far enough from the Seelie border not to be spotted, but not too far into the city's heart as to widen her search too much and lose the two of them. Each whispered conversation that carries on the breeze she follows to its source. Finally, two voices take her where she wants to go.

Cass and the vampire stand half-way down a side street. A few lights set high into the brick cast a sickly yellow light down on them, a highlight against the shadows. The two turn toward Flora as she approaches. She takes a few steps down the street before she leans against the wall.

Flora laughs, the sound of it echoing against the bricks. "I can't believe it," she says. "I truly can't." But it's not long before her laughter turns to tears. Her head falls and her free hand covers her face, her shoulders slumping.

"Flora!" Cassie takes an involuntary step toward her, hand reaching out.

Kierian approaches Flora, gently moving past Cassie. His steps are even, measured, but she doesn't look up. He stops a short distance from her, waiting quietly. He speaks as the space between her sobs grows.

"We made it out," Kierian says. "We have you to thank for that, but we can't stay here. You said you needed our help. You promised to give us yours. We're no good to each other if we're arrested or worse. Let me get us someplace safe to rest. Then we can figure out where to go from here so we can keep our promises."

Flora brushes the tears away before looking up at Kierian. "You have somewhere to go?"

Kierian lets out a short, rueful laugh. "Not that I would go in any other circumstance," he says. "But I can think of a few places we won't be found."

Flora composes herself, pushing off from the wall and standing to her full height. "Lead the way."

Chapter 9

KIERIAN NEVER UNDERSTOOD THE purpose of setting up protected spots scattered throughout the city. They haven't served a purpose since the last war between the mythics. Long centuries have gone by where even if peace isn't the most accurate word, it's at least relatively close. Still, even if these spots are a remnant of an earlier time, Kierian remembers one that's roughly halfway between the seelie territory and his clan. As far as he's aware, only the vampires know its location. Hopefully, they don't run across anyone else - seelie, vampire, or otherwise.

Kierian guides them toward an older section of the city where some of the original architecture still stands, if only as decoration for the higher stories of buildings. There's history to these streets. He's been told all the stories, which bricks were laid by what kind of hands, but it didn't mean much to him at the time. He can't recall most of it either. But the important details, like the hideout he's looking for, he can still remember.

In a wall adjacent to a church, a statue stands in an alcove. She's taller than all of them, but the statue's head is bowed in prayer, her hands folded. Her face is hard to distinguish as age has weathered her form. Moss and other small plants hang to the details and cracks that remain. Kierian has always liked this spot. There's a sort of peace that lingers here. He still can't find the words to describe it, but he lets the feeling wash over him.

"This is it," Kierian says. "Just let me get it open."

He moves behind the statue, running his hand along the stones that line the alcove. The texture of one stone is off. He pauses, feeling it again. That's what he's looking for. Kierian digs at the edges of the stone, searching for worn grooves from hands long gone. Or maybe not, depending on who they belonged to. It's wedged deep but he finally pulls it free. He turns it over in his hand. The back of the stone is hollowed out in the center.

A small lever mechanism is revealed in the wall's gap. Kierian pulls it, and off to one side, though he can't see its source, something clicks. A portion of the wall slowly pulls back inside of the alcove. Kierian presses it gently. The hinges squeal with age. He covers the lever with the stone again, then opens the door.

"Come on, quickly," Kierian says. His eyes scan the vacant street, aware of every sound nearby. "We need to get this shut fast." He waits until they've both passed through and is sure no one is watching to enter.

Kierian shuts the door, the squealing of hinges setting his teeth on edge. He presses the door back into the wall. There's another click off to one side and when Kierian tests it the door stays shut.

Kierian scans the perimeter of the space. He makes note of where Cassie and Flora stand. The main room has the bare necessities required to identify a kitchen and a living room. So far, they're alone. In the far corner there are two closed doors. Kierian treads lightly across the space, approaching each one. He enters the rooms one at a time, his hands in fists and at the ready, but both the bedroom and equally rudimentary bathroom are unoccupied beyond furniture. As he returns to the main room, it's Cassie's uneven breathing that he notices the most.

Kierian crosses the room toward her, stopping a few feet from her. "Are you okay?"

Cassie jumps, her eyes seeming to look right over him before settling on his right shoulder. "I can't see anything."

"Light! Sorry, let me fix that." Embarrassment courses through him. He quickly reaches for the nearest wall to search for any source of light. He might not need it but that doesn't mean it's not important.

In a box near the door, Kierian uncovers a few flashlights and an electric lantern next to a pile of batteries. They're all covered in dust. When Kierian clicks on the lantern, it glows. For a few minutes, an orb of light is burned into Kierian's vision every time he blinks.

Kierian rummages through the rest of the storage in the kitchen. Pulling out cabinets and drawers, he finds a few different things. One contains blood in glass jars. They appear thick and dark, almost like jam. Kierian shuts that drawer very quickly, drawing the attention of his two companions.

"Is everything okay?" Cassie says.

Despite his best efforts, Kierian glances down at the closed drawer again. His hand is still closed around the handle. He takes a step back, forcing himself to let go and look back at Cassie. "There's no food in that one," he says. Neither one of them question him, but he promises himself not to open it again.

Kierian does scavenge some granola bars and, oddly enough, chocolate. He hands some of each to Cassie and Flora. "It's the best

I can do for now," he says. "Hopefully, it will be enough for the time being. It looks like if we clear out this place, we'll have enough to last for handful of days."

"Days?" There's a pitch of distress in Cassie's voice. Her face is set into a frown, but whenever she relaxes even slightly her eyelids start to flutter shut.

"I don't plan to be here for days," Kierian says. "But we do need rest. Then we can find your sister."

"Find her sister?" Flora says.

"Yes," Kierian says. "The short version is I'm relatively sure my clan has her. My plan so far is to create a distraction that will allow the two of you to gain entry into the enclave. I should be able to draw enough attention that no one stops either of you from finding Cass' sister. After that, we can all escape."

Cassie leans forward slightly, her eyes narrowed at him. "What's your distraction?"

Kierian fights to keep his expression neutral. What he's less confident about is whether he can keep his voice even as well.

"Kier?" Cassie says. "What's your plan for a distraction."

"I'm going to give them exactly what they're looking for," Kierian says. "The building should be empty if they call their court to order. Empty besides the two of you and your sister."

Kierian can feel Flora's eyes on him, but she says nothing. Her silence keeps him composed, focusing on Cassie.

"But you're escaping with us, right?" Cassie says.

"That's the plan," Kierian says. He'd like to make it out alive, but making a promise he doesn't have the power to keep isn't too far from a lie in his eyes. So, he answers how he can.

"We're all making it out," Cassie says. Her voice is firm, no room for argument. He can tell she wants to believe it. He wants to believe it too, but there's not the same certainty within him. If Flora and Cassie find her sister and make it out, he's willing to pay whatever the price may be for them to get away.

***

Cassie stares up at the ceiling. Even with the blankets pulled up to her neck, a chill clings tightly to Cassie's skin. Her mind won't stop racing. She can't lose her sister. Every fiber of her being clings to those five words. She has no idea what that loss would do to her and she hopes against all odds she never has to find out. The more she clings to that hope verging on desperation, the more she starts to realize she doesn't want to lose Kierian either.

Now that she's awake, Cassie can't fall back asleep again. She slips quietly out of bed. Her feet hit the ground with a soft noise as she pads toward the door. Flora is asleep in a chair in the corner, but Cassie can't make out her form. Everything is dark. Cassie keeps one hand out in front of her. There's not enough space or clutter for her to really worry about running into anything, but she can't help it. The only exception would be the locked dresser. None of them tried to open it, and for that she's thankful. Cassie narrows her eyes in its general direction before opening the bedroom door.

She steps out into the living room, letting the door close softly behind her. She's more careful now not to bump into anything. As Cassie runs a hand along the back of the couch, she can just make out the back of Kierian's head over a chair. She pauses then, caught between letting him sleep or calling his name. Before she can decide, the bedroom door swings open again.

Cassie looks back the direction she came, the darkness taking a fuzzy form. "Flora?"

"Good morning," Flora says. Her voice drifts across the dark space. "Mid-morning if I had to guess."

Cassie starts to ask how she knows that but settles on a different question instead. "You know what we need you for," she says. "Why do you need us?" Cassie squints against the darkness, but she still can't quite see the fae.

"What do you know about the fae courts?" Flora says.

"There's more than one?"

"Two of them, to be exact." The warmth in her tone calms some of Cassie's nerves. It also draws her in, learning more about this world she's now a part of. "To give the story of everything from the beginning might be helpful, but I don't believe we have the time. There is the seelie and the unseelie court. You've seen one, the one that used to claim me. We stand opposed, mostly in the way we view humanity, imprints, and the rules we follow. We're also in an agreement of peace. Each time a court calls a meeting the other court sends two representatives to take part in overseeing the proceedings. I used to be one of them. We didn't have any political power but it meant there weren't any secrets being kept. Our peace accords called for knowledge of truth on both sides.

"There's never been a reason for either side to close their doors, not as long as I've been alive. The only problem with those accords, in my eyes, is what happens if those representatives are denied entry. A few cycles ago I was stopped at the unseelie gates. There wasn't anything we could do to gain entry if it was denied to us. It takes at least three rejections to allow an investigation. In the space between those rejections, though, years can pass. I didn't want to take the risk that something would happen before we could lift a finger against it. So, I found my own way inside."

Flora pauses. The warmth in her voice shifts to something just shy of tempered anger. There's a dull edge to her words, as if she's repeated them enough times when they're finally spoken aloud they're almost too refined.

"When I got back to my court, I told them what happened. They were more upset that I went inside anyway, claiming no matter what information I brought back they couldn't do anything with. That meeting wasn't mine to know, much less relay. So, they turned my warning out and left me to continue as I always had."

Cassie tries to listen as she moves around to the front of the couch and sinks down into it. "What did you find?" Cassie says.

"The unseelie don't see imprinting as anything more than a tool," Flora says. There's an edge of anger to her voice, sharp and bitter. "They'll take what they want, use what they need, and then throw it away to continue with whatever they were doing before. They don't care what broken things they leave in their wake. If they want to start a war, which I think they do, the first thing they need is to raise an army. To them, an army of imprints is an army of disposables."

Kierian shifts in the chair. His voice catches Cassie off guard. "You're going to try and stop a war with only us to help? I thought my plan was fragile. Hearing yours, I think we might just be able to pull it off."

Flora shakes her head. "I don't need to stop a war," she says. "I just need to know how it's going to happen. If the seelie won't listen, nothing I could ever bring to them will change their mind. I don't imagine fighting the unseelie court face to face or directly will have a pleasant outcome. The only way to minimize casualties is to start fighting at the roots. Understanding what their plan is means we can thwart their means of revelation. Protect the humans we can, persuade those that are being used. If we wait until their plans of revelation are unfolding, until they've raised their army, it's too late. That kind of damage can't be undone. If they're going to try and shake the foundations of everything, we need know what we're up against."

"You're only trying and stop the Unseelie from raising an army?" Kierian says. "It doesn't sound much saner when you put it like that."

Cassie frowns. She doesn't disagree, but there's something in Flora's words that keeps coming back to her. Something that reminds her of Kierian. "If it only saves one life..." she starts. There's no way for her to finish that sentence. She's not sure where it leads, but the bond ripples slightly.

"If it only saves one life..." Kierian says quietly. He doesn't finish the sentence either. It's left hanging in mid-air as he turns toward her. She can't read his expression in the dark, though she can see his outline now. A few more moments of silence pass before Kierian speaks.

"I forgot about the light!" he says. He jumps into motion, quickly scaling the back of the chair so he can reach the lantern. Cassie can't help but laugh at the sight of him when he grimaces because he forgets to close his eyes, the light coming on just inches from his face again.

Chapter 10

THE THREE OF THEM leave the safe haven almost exactly as they found it. Only the drawer with the old jars of blood remains wholly untouched. Kierian closes the door in the wall behind them. It seals with a sense of finality. They won't be coming back here again.

At the height of the day, the lull of the sun's heat means most of their vampiric resistance is inside, not keeping perimeter watches. Kierian can feel the warmth radiating through him. Having the sun in his eyes makes it slightly less enjoyable.

Kierian leads, focusing his footsteps to avoid most of the sunlight and forcing himself to keep moving. His thoughts are unruly. He can't tune them out completely. As much as he'd like to not meet his end today, there's so much outside of his control it's hard to say what's going to happen once they get inside that compound. He's not particularly looking forward to returning.

The air shifts as they approach the edges of his clan's land. Their territory isn't as deeply set in history as the fae's is, so the lines within the earth are closer to the surface. More able to be moved. Still, he can feel the weight of crossing over. Familiar scents draw him in, his sense of direction grounded even more in the physical space around him.

Even as danger fills the gaps of his senses, he can't help but smile. This is not his home, but he's about to make a homecoming entrance.

Flora and Cassie stay behind as he approaches the bar. He walks right across the threshold, nodding at the bartender. An exhilarating mix of adrenaline and dread drags its way slowly through Kierian's veins. He's not walking into a wolf's den. He's walking into something much, much worse.

A few tables are occupied by various kinds of mythics. Even though it's only been a year, his eyes skim over the different eyes, jaws, colors, and other not-so-human anomalies until he finds what he's looking for. He spots the one table of vampires, this time situated in the back of the room. With the smallest of movements, he bears the tips of his fangs at them. Then he makes his way toward the door just past the bar. Chairs scrape behind him. Kierian doesn't look back as he passes the bar and opens the door into the heart of his clan's territory.

Kierian goes through the door and turns right down the hallway. The wide double doors of the meeting room are closed. There must be something important going on in there, otherwise it would be empty and the doors open. Hopefully, it's not more important than this.

The enclave building used to be a small performing arts center. Most of the wings have been renovated but the performance hall remains untouched. A stage curves out along the left side of the room. Seats fan out in a semi-circular pattern facing the stage. Set backdrops still litter the stage, hiding what used to be cast entrances. Kierian's pretty sure now they're covered in dust and other things he'd like to not think about.

Only about a quarter of the audience is full. There's two faces Kierian recognizes, though, both standing up on stage. They're right at home there. He can't help but smile as they look over at him, though there's no warmth in it.

Kierian steps inside the room, extending his arms out at his sides. "I believe you've been looking for me," he says.

Pryor moves first. He pushes past a few other vampires on the stage, appearing more clearly in Kierian's vision as he stands on the edge of the stage. It takes Pryor a second too long to conceal his surprise and Kierian catches his wide-eyed stare. The voice that breaks the silence doesn't belong to either of them.

"You came at just the right time. If we couldn't resolve this situation soon we were going to have to call our council to meeting."

Emrys. His face remains impassive as always. They've moved away from titles like kings and nobles, but a king is what he would be. And he's no figurehead either. Kierian can still remember the first time he was in this room. It was the first choice he had to make as a new vampire: align himself with the clan that had changed him or go out on his own. Going out on his own was the ill-advised option. It would make him a target, at least that's what they told him. And so, he made the only choice he thought he had at the time.

He didn't realize they only told him fragments of the truth. He found out later, when with each passing day it became more dangerous to leave than to stay. Even now it's hard to tell what he really believes and what lies they've spoken he thinks are truth.

Emrys was standing over him the first time. Emrys is still on the stage, but this time Kierian is appearing in front of the council on his own terms. Whatever choice he makes here will not be one of necessity or desperation.

"When I saw the doors closed, I thought I might find you here, Emrys," Kierian says, bowing slightly. "You should still probably call the council."

"For what purpose?" Emrys asks. "There's no shortage of matters to attend to. What makes yours so special?" There's a flat inquisitiveness to his voice. It takes all of Kierian's self-control to speak calmly.

"I'm in violation of the clan's statues," Kierian says. "I haven't followed your rules. My imprint is still alive, and I have no intention of turning her."

Kierian doesn't break Emrys' stare. Bodies shift in the theatre seats, but he's not worried about a single one of them. Only Emrys' reaction can cause the distraction he wants. Only Emrys can give Cassie and Flora the cover to get in and out. Kierian might be the distraction, but it's the court itself that will provide the means to let Cassie's sister go free.

"Persuade me why I shouldn't simply deal with you right now," Emrys says. "Why draw it out when we can be finished in just a few moments?"

Kierian walks further into the room, approaching the side of the stage. Pryor sneers at him. The other vampire is safe from momentary reproof while Emrys can't see his face. Kierian ignores him, focusing all his attention on Emrys.

"If I may be so bold," Kierian says. "I would argue that is not how you solve problems in this court. You can address more than one issue at a time if dealt with in the right way. What better cure could walk into your hands than a new vampire who doesn't want to follow your rules? One that you made."

Emrys walks toward Kierian slowly, his gait demanding attention in subtle motions. He stops at the edge of the stage, towering over Kierian. He crouches, his head just a few feet above Kierian.

"I don't like giving people exactly what they want," Emrys says. "You've evaded our court admirably. You stand here alone is testament to that. I'm inclined to meet your request on two conditions. First, you will answer all the questions I ask about her. Second, Pryor oversees the proceedings. From calling the court to the administration of justice, it will be in his hands. I reserve the right to overrule any decision, so you may make your case to me at any time, but I make no promises. After all, the purpose of this is to make an example of the new vampire who has held the accords of this clan in contempt, especially since he's one I made."

The price of his distraction starts to settle on Kierian's shoulders. Emrys is giving him what he asked for in the least pleasant way. Then again, he didn't really expect anything different. Pryor is one of the last, possibly the very last, he would want to be in charge of something like this. That's the point. Kierian has to play by the rules that are given to him. He didn't come here to turn himself in for the fun of it. Emrys is smarter than to be fooled by that. Kierian is going to have to earn every minute he provides for Cassie and Flora. For Vivian.

"Thank you," Kierian says. "I can submit to those conditions."

Emrys smiles, standing up. "Come up on stage then, Kierian," he says. "Today you're the star of the show."

***

Flora and Cassie wait around a corner, just out of sight of the bar. The first time she was here Cassie didn't know what she was getting herself into. Now that she knows behind that through the alley and the bar is a vampire lair, it takes all Cassie's strength to hold her resolve. She's walking into it, knowing what's beyond those walls. She has to remind herself to breathe.

Without warning, an overwhelming weight presses down on her shoulders. Instead of the bond drawing her toward Kierian, it seems to compress around her waist, holding her in place. "Are you okay?" She can hear Flora's voice, but it sounds further away than she should. "Can you talk to me? What's going on."

Cass takes a deep breath. "I can't move. I don't know if it's me or not. It's like something is trying to suffocate me."

Cassie gasps. A familiar heat breaks out along the bond, stemming from Kierian and rushing toward her. It pulses in synch with her heartbeat, growing faster as her breaths come quicker. It's the same feeling as when he bared his fangs leaving the seelie sector, when he had to bring himself back from the edge of becoming something else.

"I don't think he's okay." It takes all Cassie's strength to whisper those words. The shift in his eyes flashes through her mind. He's changing.

Cassie squeezes her eyes shut, breathing as deeply as she possibly can. "I have to save her. That's the point. All of this is meant to save her."

Flora speaks softly. "We don't have much time, especially if that's how you're feeling. I have to assume that's the signal. We need to go now."

Cassie nods. The turmoil of their bond doesn't still but she can breathe regularly. She takes one step, then another.

"Stay close," Flora says. Cassie takes two unsteady steps after Flora, her gait evening out as she follows.

Cassie recognizes the troll behind the bar as they pass through the faux wall. His big eyes get even wider, but he quickly looks away. In that same moment, though, he knocks two full drinks over. The glass shatters at the far side of the bar, drawing the attention of the patrons still inside. She's not sure if he did it on purpose, but she mirrors Flora's quick, darting movement behind the bar and through the door just past it. The door clicks shut, dulling the shouts that rise behind them.

Flora scans the dim hallway. There are large decorative doors to their right. Light trickles out from underneath it, sounds muffled from that direction. Flora still lifts a finger to her lips then starts down the hall away from those doors.

Cassie glances over her shoulder, the tension of the bond growing the further she walks away from those doors. Kierian must be in there. Filing that information away, first she needs to find her sister. Then they'll get Kierian out of here.

Cassie tries to recall the layout Kierian described, but the most she can do is stay close to Flora and hope the fae remembers. A larger hallway opens to their right and they turn down it. Here, doors locked on the outside line the walls, small distances between them. It's as if a hotel block doubled the number of rooms in one hallway. Small little plaques hang on the doors themselves above the handles.

Cassie studies the first sign. It's marked with two letters: HB. The metal is marred deeply. No care or attention was used to create these, just sheer force. The door across from it is marked with a VB. The same pattern repeats down the rest of the hall. On her left everything starts with a V. On the right everything starts with an H.

"Flora." It's a whisper, but Cassie's voice echoes down the hall. As Flora turns toward her, other voices start to rise from the rooms. Most are small and fragile but others begin to shout. Cassie's heartbeat races. If they don't find Vivian soon, she's not sure what will happen. Cassie only has one idea. It means giving away her name and her sister's, but that's a risk Cassie is willing to take if it means finding her.

"Cassie?" she calls. "Cassie, are you there?"

Immediately the sound of voices grows. Shouts of "I'm here!" are all she can hear. All except for one. As Cassie calls her name again, quickly moving past each room, one call is different.

"Vivian." Her voice is weak, but Cassie stops at that door. The letters VB are etched into it.

"Cassie?" she says, quieter this time.

She's met with another soft call. "Vivian."

Cassie squeezes her eyes shut hard, putting a hand on the door. Her sister is on the other side, she's certain of it. She's the only one who could answer that call.

Flora comes up behind her, deftly working on the latch lock system. "We can open it," she says. Cassie steps back, watching Flora work.

As soon as the lock clicks, Flora pushes the door in. A girl with dark and wild curly hair pushes past her and runs into the embrace of her sister. Cassie holds Vivian like it's the first and last time she's ever held her in her arms. It's the only way she can explain it. Everything in her chest wants to explode and she can't let go.

"We can't stay here," Flora says. Her voice is louder now, having to be heard above the rising noise that continues to grow despite their cries not being answered. Cassie holds on to Vivian a bit tighter, feeling her sister squeeze in response. It's not nearly long enough before Cassie pulls back enough to see Vivian's face. Those eyes wide eyes stare back at her, body trembling slightly.

"I am not going to leave you," Cassie says. "I promise. This is Flora, and she's on our side. We need to get out of here. Can you walk?"

The question racks her heart, watching her sister take a deep breath and steady herself. "I think so."

It breaks Cassie's heart how fragile that answer is, but she pulls herself together. She takes Vivian's hand and holds on tight. "Don't let go of me," Cassie says.

Chapter 11

VIVIAN'S LEGS SHAKE UNDERNEATH her. Using Cassie as a counterbalance, she's able to keep up with her sister's pace. Her gaze never leaves the ground. It's the only thing she can focus on. That, and the silents words on her lips that don't stop until they've passed every other door in the hallway: I'm sorry.

She can't close her eyes. If she closes her eyes, she's right back in the darkness.

The more Vivian moves, the tighter something else holds her. Her stomach wrenches, turning over inside her. Sweat beads on her forehead and runs down her back. Her sister's hand, Cassie's hand, is the only thing that grounds her. The inside of her shoes are damp, squishing and wet each time she takes a step. It makes her want to escape her skin.

"What's wrong?" Cassie says. If she answers that question truthfully and fully, Vivian is almost sure she'll crumble into something unrecognizable. Broken. Unable to be put back together.

"It's harder to breathe," Vivian says. "The further we walk, the tighter it holds me."

"What's holding onto you tighter?"

"I don't know." Vivian shakes her head. The warm, sticky feeling won't leave her. "It hasn't gone away since I got here."

"I think it's her imprint." Flora. Vivian remembers her name, but it's more than she wants to know.

"Just hold on," Cassie says. "We're going to get out of here and then I can tell you everything I know. I just need you to stay with me."

Vivian nods. She can hold on. She's been doing that ever since she woke up to fangs - every moment since this nightmare began. She's not exactly sure how long it's been, or what parts of herself are left. Pinch marks litter her palms and arms. If she was going to wake up she would have already.

She can just see the bottom edge of a door when a loud shout echoes down the hall. Vivian freezes, every muscle in her body tightening. It's her sister's hand loosening from hers that causes Vivian to look up. Cassie's eyes are directed down the hall toward two looming, dark doors. Vivian turns to look, her frown deepening. Whatever is trying to hold her here, it's coming from that direction too.

"I can't leave him," Cassie says. Her eyes are still fixed ahead. "Something is happening in there. I can't leave him."

There's a hand on Vivian's shoulder. She recoils from it, and the light pressure lifts. Her eyes snap toward the owner. Large, round eyes with shimmering irises, hard lines on her face, and a color to her veins. Flora is not one of them. She's something else.

"Can you tell me where the tightness you mentioned is coming from?" Flora says.

Vivian nods. "There."

"Thank you." Flora turns to her sister. "That's where they all are. Whatever distraction he's causing has bought us the time we needed but we have to trust him to get himself out. That was the plan. We-Are you listening to me?"

Cassie gasps, stumbling forward a step. Vivian tentatively moves toward her. "Cassie?" Vivian can't hold back the trembling anymore. Her sister's movements are concentrated, as if trying to resist something dragging her down the hall. Vivian's heart drops. She recognizes those signs. "You feel it too, don't you?"

Worry creases Cassie's face. She puts both hands on Vivian's shoulders, meeting her gaze. "I do," Cassie says. "I can't lose you again. I want you to know that with absolute certainty. But there's someone else who needs my help too, and I can't ignore him. I've trusted Flora with my life so she could help me find you. I need you to stay with her until I come out."

Vivian shakes her head hard. She's not in the dark anymore, she's not trapped, but it still feels like she's falling. "I won't leave you. I won't."

"I will come back to you," Cassie says. She moves one hand to Vivian's cheek, stilling her shaking. "I will. With everything I have in me, I am telling you that I will."

"But you don't know." Vivian's voice is whisper, breaking on that last word.

"I found you, didn't I?" Cassie says. "I can do it again."

"I'm not leaving without you," Vivian says.

"Stay here with Flora," Cassie says. "I will come back. I won't leave here without you either, I promise."

There aren't any words that could create a balm powerful enough to soothe the open wounds of Vivian's heart. She's not even sure what all of them are, if she was even brave enough to name them. If she even has the words to name them. But as much as she hates to let her sister go, even as exhaustion sinks into her bones, she'll hold on as long as it takes if she gets to see Cassie's face again.

***

Blood covers the front of the stage. Cut bags lie tossed to one side, their contents emptied to create this ghastly scene. It wouldn't be as much of a problem if they hadn't doused him too. That's what makes the instinct so hard to control. Both hands cuffed to the front row of audience seats doesn't make things any easier either.

Pryor leans toward him from the bloody stage, fangs bared in a cold smile. "Good so far, Kierian," Pryor says. "Just keep pulling her toward you. Once she's here we can call for the court's decision. Though, we already know what their verdict is going to be, don't we? Your first imprint, and your first taste of fresh blood. Exciting, isn't it?"

Kierian bucks against the restraint, a physical reaction he can't control. His wrists are red and chaffed. If he's bleeding too, he can't tell. He squeezes his eyes shut, leaning away from the stage, but he can't get far enough. He can feel the blood covering him, his skin sticky, clothes plastered to him, hair matted. Her heartbeat races along their bond.

His fangs press hard against his bottom lip. He can feel the impulse to allow himself to shift in every inch of his body. His pupils changing, the quickening of his usually inanimate pulse. There's a rush of chemicals trying to drag themselves through his bloodstream, tempting him to feel something.

She's only getting closer. He can feel the distance closing. He's known all along she wasn't that far away. After all, that was the whole purpose of this plan. But now he's drawing her right into their hands. Everything he's done so far to spare her of this fate will be in vain if she doesn't make it out of here unscathed by fangs.

The double doors open and his eyes dart toward the movement. His thoughts race, but for the first time in what seems like an antagonizing forever, he holds still. Because there she is. Hair falling past her shoulders, eyes finding his, hands clasped in front of her. She's standing off to the side of the stage and the audience, the whole scene to survey. Kierian's attention is solely on her.

"Welcome. We were hoping you would make an appearance," Pryor says. The way he smiles at Cassie sends a murderous impulse through Kierian he hardly wants to contain. It's what's little is left of Kierian's dignity that keeps him standing mostly upright.

Cassie steps into the room alone, the door closing behind her. Her movements are tentative, but she keeps approaching, finding her way to the stage steps on the far side of the room. His thoughts are screaming, but as much as he doesn't want her to see him like this, doesn't want her to see him at all, he can't take his eyes off her. If she kept walking along the semi-circle of the stage, she'd end up right in front of him. Kierian shakes his head, trying to get that image out of his head.

It's when she cries out, hands closing around her, that his blissful moment of stillness is shattered. It takes all the self-control Kierian has left to restrain himself, including reminding himself of the cuffs. There's a chance he could get loose, but whether his hands or the chair would break first is a calculation he's not able to make right now. The distant desire to still have functioning hands after this, if there is an after, wins out.

"Keep your hands off her." Kierian hardly recognizes his own voice.

Laughter echoes from the crowd behind him. Pryor, hands still on Cassie, pulls her up the stage steps. He leads her along the edge of the stage until they're standing in front of Kierian. Pryor's rougher than he needs to be with her. Kierian can't tell that she's resisting, only that she's staring at him. Her lips are parted and unmoving. He can't look away from her.

"We'll keep things civil. This is, after all, our court of law," Pryor says. Kierian can see the outline of him close behind Cassie, holding her hands behind her back.

Kierian rattles the cuffs. "Civil. I'd hate to see what an uncivilized proceeding looks like."

"We've hardly begun," Pryor says. "Your first choice, option one." Before he can continue, Kierian shakes his head.

"No."

"You didn't let me finish," Pryor says. There's almost a tinge of pride in his voice, though Kierian shutters to imagine what the object of that pride is. "Your resistance is admirable. You've held out longer than most of us would. But then, we're not all the same, are we? Option one, we bring her down there and you can turn her yourself."

Pryor's smile turns to a sneer. In a swift motion he kicks the back of Cassie's knees. Kierian sways at the force of it, though it's not just the physical echo of Cassie's pain. It's watching Pryor bring her to a kneeling and then crouching behind her. It's no longer just her shoes covered in blood. Now it's seeping up the fabric of her pants. She's still staring at him, wide eyes and lips parted.

"Kierian."

The first time he hears it, he can't be certain she actually says his name. The second time he sees her lips move.

"Kierian."

"Let her go," Kierian says. This time he doesn't try and resist the growl in his voice.

Pryor enunciates each word, his face just above Cassie's shoulder, his fangs unhidden. "Option one."

"You would have to kill me first," Kierian says.

Pryor smiles, one hand reaching for the sheath at his waist. "Gladly, if you insist..."

Emry's hands close on Kierian's shoulders. "He still has his rights," Emrys says. "And she is still his imprint. Don't forget your place in this court. Blood may still be shed, but there's more than one outcome to this proceeding."

Pryor frowns but doesn't argue. "Option two," he says. "Start with her name. What is it?"

"Not for you to ever say." Kierian spits the words. A small amount of saliva hits the ground and mixes with dark, crimson blood.

"Kierian. You'll answer the question. What is her name?" Emry's voice is sweet, carrying a lightness to it. Kierian learned long ago, though, that sweetness is always poised just before a knife. He bears a scar in remembrance of that, one he'll keep her from carrying if he can do anything about it.

"Cassie." Kierian has to force her name from his lips. "Her name is Cassie."

"Cassie," Pryor says. "How sweet. That's a lovely name, but you know that's not really option two, don't you Kierian?"

"Don't threaten her," Kierian says, but now he's staring at the knife poised at her torso, held in Pryor's hand.

"I'm not threatening anyone. This is a civil court," Pryor says. "Option two. If you won't turn her then we release her."

"Again, you'll have to release me, kill me, first," Kierian says. "You won't lay a hand on her before then."

Pryor's other hand shifts, still gripping Cassie's shoulder. "It's a bit too late for that," he says.

"He is your brother," Emrys says. Kierian isn't sure whether that remark is meant for him or Pryor. "However, this arrangement isn't getting us anywhere. I assume, Kierian, if you have refused the first two rights that the third, allowing someone else to turn her, would also be less preferable than death. The girl is here. Everything is in place and we're not leaving until something is done. Let's deal with this more maturely. I trust both of you can conduct yourselves with dignity?"

Emrys inserts the key to the cuffs, and the metal clicks as they release. Kierian pulls his hands free, taking one step forward. He locks eyes with Pryor, the imprint burning through him.

"I can conduct myself with dignity," Kierian says. His words trail off as he stretches his freed hands and wrists. It's painful, but they still function like they should. "Before we continue, though there's just one thing I need you to know, Pryor. I am not your brother."

He might be a danger to everyone in this room, but there's nothing holding him back anymore. Kierian leaps forward, reaching for the edge of the stage. Cassie cries out. A gun is fired, the shot cutting through the room, followed by a large crash. Flora bursts through a play backdrop made of a thin sheet of wood, designed to break at a significant amount of force. There's an outline of her person in the wood as she grins wildly. The barrel of a gun sweeps across the stage until it levels at Pryor.

All the noise from the theatre hall quiets. There's only one wet slap as Kierian grips the edge of the stage, just a few feet from Cassie. In all the blood, Pryor lost his grip on her as he scrambled to his feet. Cassie still kneels, her hands at her side.

"They'll both be coming with me," Flora says. Her voice is the last intelligible sound before the whole room erupts.

Kierian pulls himself onto the stage. Cassie scrambles back from him. He has to sit there for a moment, waiting for the fire in his muscles to relent so he can stand. A hand closes around his ankle, causing him to slip backward the way he came.

"Go!" Kierian says. Cassie disappears from his sight, and he can only hope it's toward where Flora came from. Kierian loses his grip on the stage. He kicks at the figure behind him, landing one blow, only for more hands to close in on him. He's pulled back into the audience, landing hard on the ground. Pain lances through his body. Another shot rings out, ringing in his ears as he swings at every moving thing. It's only as his back is against the stage that a circle starts to clear around him. A shadow looms over him, and Kierian looks up.

Flora stands above him, a pistol quickly sweeping to keep the crowd of vampires around him at bay. "You see the position we're in?" she says.

"I do," Kierian says. He grabs the edge of the stage, pulling himself up. There's another shot and this time it's close enough the ringing shatters his hearing for a minute. Flora grabs him, dragging them stumbling across the stage and behind the set Flora broke through. Kierian only gets a shaky look at the scene before it's gone.

"Don't forget who made you!" Emrys' words send a spike through Kierian's heart. He can still remember how the vampire's eyes changed, but the look in his eyes never did. An insatiable hunger. Kierian thought he was going to die at that moment. Kierian thought he was going to die every moment in between seeing those fangs, trapped in a dark room, and covered in his own blood on this stage. Instead, he's been left alive, haunted by every moment he's still been allowed to live, no breath in him.

"How could I ever forget?" Kierian says. The words aren't for anyone but himself.

Kierian ducks through the hole in the set, following Flora. In the dim, narrow hallway, Cassie embraces her sister. Kierian only catches a glimpse of wild, curly hair while Cassie stands between him and Vivian. He closes his eyes. He tries to listen to Flora's quick set of instructions but it's not enough to distract him. Instead, he focuses on things that aren't covered in blood. The edge of Cassie's sleeve, the hem of her shirt, the set Flora destroyed. The top of Cassie's head, probably. He pulls himself back from the edge he never wanted to discover in himself, the edge that they created in him, clawing back as much as he can reclaim of himself.

It's Flora repeating his name that shocks him enough to pull him back. "Kierian! I need you to take the lead. Cassie, you and your sister stay close to him. I'll pick up the rear in case any of them want to see how many shots I have left. But we need to move now!"

Kierian's steps are unsteady at first, but he quickly regains his footing. There's still enough adrenaline in him that the pain isn't overwhelming yet. He just needs to think. They won't have enough time to make it out through the bar. That exit will already be covered, he's sure of it. If they can make it just a bit further, though, there's another exit. Not as hidden as the bar, but he can deal with problems as they come. There's only so many he can anticipate. They need to survive. If they can accomplish that, they can deal with the rest later. They're in the cast hallways, filled with dressing rooms and prop closets. Just a little further and he'll find the emergency exit meant for the long-passed cast.

Kierian makes a few quick turns, then pulls a door open at the end of a shallow corridor. He steps through, quickly scanning the surroundings before letting the other three come out. People on the street pass by them but no one stares. No one even notices them. The wooden flooring beneath their feet gives away the fact they're not out in the open.

Only a few buildings have these connected passages. Kierian likens them to skywalks, though they're on the ground and not in the air. This hallway, built by some type of mythic hands, connects them to a few different paths they could take. Given the fact most of the four of them are covered in blood, it makes the most sense to stay within the confines of the hall. Up ahead, the hallway comes to a four-way crossroad. Kierian just can't remember where each path is supposed to take them. Still, Kierian leads them forward, his mind spinning. Mythics pass, crossing the seal in the center of the junction. None of them pay extra attention to the four of them. There are stranger things than the sight of them, he's sure. Not many, but a few.

Just as they reach the seal, a hand clasps Kierian's shoulder. Kierian jumps, his hands closing into fists as he turns sharply toward the touch. A mythic stands next to him, bug eyed with reddish-brown veins and too-white teeth. They're marks of a seelie fae, as far as Kierian can tell. The hand on his shoulder is released as Kierian steps between the fae and the other three.

"Do you need something?" Kierian says. "We don't have much time to spare."

The fae shrugs. "Not particularly. Though, it seems more appropriate for me to ask if you all need something. I think it's safe to assume you all need somewhere to go that's not back to where you came from."

Kierian studies the fae, mostly in an attempt to gain a little more time. There doesn't appear to be any malice in his words or body language. There's no obvious weapon, and one not being leveled at him is a welcome enough change. They can run, but Kierian is running low on safe places they can reasonably get to. This might be the best chance they have.

"You might be right," Kierian says.

The seelie fae grins, clapping Kierian on the shoulder. "Great!" he says. "Just walk with me."

Kierian glances back at Flora. Her face is stoic, but she doesn't say anything. The fae walks alongside Kierian, his proximity putting Kierian on edge. He's careful to watch every movement. The fae leads them straight across the seal, taking a hidden lane to the back door of a tall, brick building. There's nothing out of the ordinary Kierian notices. He's not completely confident in his abilities at the moment, but Flora doesn't stop them either.

"I'm Bayler," the fae says. He opens the door to a large apartment complex, ushering them inside. "Obviously this isn't where you'll want to stay forever, but it's an in-between place I've set up and maintained for occasions like his one."

"This happens frequently?" Flora asks.

"Not so much these days," Bayler says. "You'd be surprised, or maybe not, how much things can change in a short amount of time. I used to be an independent doctor. That didn't turn out too well, mostly because of what I am. But it does mean we can get all of you cleaned up and not draw any more unwanted attention."

Kierian's gut reaction is to resist. Even following Bayler up the stairs, Kierian holds tension in his body. It's almost too easy. But they're covered in blood, tracking debris behind them, exhaustion likely to claim each of them very soon. If he were to decline, where else would they go?

Kierian glances over his shoulder once they reach the landing. Vivian folds herself into Cassie's arms as they wait for Bayler to unlock the room door. It's at that sight his heart begins to melt. They need rest. They have each other, but they might still have a long way to go. He hasn't had enough time to feel how tired he is himself.

"Here we are," Bayler says. The door swings open without a sound. "Whatever you need is yours. All you have to do is ask."

Kierian hesitates before stepping over the threshold. He never wanted to set foot in a fae residence of his own free will, but things have changed more rapidly than he ever could have expected. "Thank you," Kierian says. "May I come inside?"

Bayler smiles. "You may."

Chapter 12

ALL THEIR BLOODY ARTICLES of clothing sit in a bag just inside the door. Bayler's stash had enough clothes to fit them once they cleaned most of the blood off themselves. Kierian can hear the other shower still running down the hall.

Cassie peers around the corner every few minutes, never leaving her post in front of the bathroom door. Vivian is still in there. He can't tell if the splotches of red on Cassie's skin are blood or if she's rubbing her skin so hard it's becoming irritated. She shakes her head every time he starts to get up, disappearing back behind the corner. It's only Bayler and Flora's conversation that keeps him sane as he tries to wait.

"I know you don't have to tell me," Bayler says. "But I am more than a little curious about what happened back there." There's an ease to his words. Bayler leans back into the couch but his quickly shifting gaze is alert, attentive. One thumb taps continuously despite his interlaced hands.

Kierian catches Flora's quick glance. They have to be careful what they tell him. Without knowing more about this fae they can't risk giving anything away that could be used against them.

"Thank you for your hospitality," Flora says. "We certainly needed it. However, if you're content for us to rest here before sending us off, knowing the details of how we got here isn't going to do you much good."

"If you're worried about putting me in danger you can rest assured I've seen more troubled situations than this," Bayler says. "I've managed to survive this long. Besides, I can already put some of the pieces together. It's hard to hide an encounter with a vampire clan and living this close to one you're not the first I've seen. If you weren't a fae, I'd almost be content to let the story be finished there."

"Why not let the story rest anyway?" Kierian says. He's having trouble distinguishing the exhaustion in his bones from Cassie's. Rest in general sounds like a wonderful plan.

Flora shoots Kierian a withering glance with enough force he wonders how she has the energy for it. "Pardon my bluntness, but why does the story matter to you?" Flora says to Bayler.

"I already told you it's in my nature to help those that I can," Bayler says. "I'm not working now, though. Without a practice, I haven't been able to help nearly as many people. That's why I'm here. I take more of a street approach to identifying people who might need help. Unsurprisingly, you four fit that criteria."

Kierian would be hard pressed to judge whether Bayler is lying. Kierian doesn't want to believe him, but the more Bayler talks, the more it feels like he's grasping at straws for reasons to distrust him.

"Are you asking to help us?" Flora says. "Beyond what you're providing to us here?" She leans forward, arms folded over her knees in the chair across from him. She holds Bayler's stare.

"That depends," Bayler says. He leans forward slightly, mirroring her posture. "What do you need help with?"

"What do you stand to gain?" Flora says.

Bayler laughs, interrupting the tense moment. "You're one of those court officials, aren't you?" Bayler says. His grin is wide. "It's fascinating even in all these years they haven't changed so much. If you're looking for a specific answer, I'm afraid I don't know what it is you want. The seelie court cut me off a long time ago. Granted, I chose to live in this world. They didn't like it, but they didn't stop me at the time. I can't imagine anyone would still care, but if you're here to question me I suppose I should be a little more professional. It's hard to care, though, at this point.

"But to your question, this is what I want. I've gained what I've built. These safe havens are what I've made, the only thing lasting from before I lost my practice. It's not the humans' faults when the world tells them they're crazy they start to believe it. It's easier than fighting to believe what they see might be real, especially when they've been used and abandoned. When your doctor looks like the monsters you've been trying to convince yourself you can't see, eventually other people start to take notice of that kind of reaction. Drawing attention to the existence of a race that's meant to exist in secret isn't looked kindly upon, at least it wasn't then."

"You don't receive news from either court?" Flora asks.

"You would be my first messenger in a long time," Bayler says with a shrug. "I can't say I'm particularly interested in anything they have to say, though you may prove me wrong."

"They're planning a mass revelation to the humans, to expose themselves and establish a kingdom outside of secrecy," Flora says. "Is that of interest to you?"

Bayler nods once. "It is. Please continue."

"I am the only outside witness," Flora says. "Even as a seelie court representative, the unseelie court did their best to prevent me entrance. I was able to get through and infiltrate their court in order to hear their plans. To the seelie, they only committed a minor infraction of the peace accords. I suppose acknowledging my testimony would mean accepting a larger infraction, but it wouldn't have mattered if they'd understood what was at stake."

"What is at stake?" Bayler says.

Flora glances at Kierian pointedly, but he shrugs. Their back and forth is more political than Kierian can understand. Whatever she's trying to stay through her stare, Kierian has no hope of understanding it without her saying something.

"The lives of innocents," Flora says. "If the unseelie court goes to war, who do you think their first target will be? The humans. Not to eliminate them, but to recruit them."

Bayler nods slowly. "So, you're trying to do something about it, since the rest of your court won't."

"I am." There's a strength to her words Kierian can't ignore. There's also that same bitter anger from before. She has passion and that's something he can't fault her for.

"You know acting on your own is yet another infraction," Bayler says.

"I know," Flora says. "That's why I'm not acting on behalf of the seelie court."

The room is quiet. The distant sound of running water ceases, leaving them with just the sound of the fae breathing.

"You asked before what I wanted, and I think I have a different answer now," Bayler says. He sits taller, the playful tone dropping from his voice. "Formally, I ask if you'd be willing to take one more with you."

Flora doesn't hesitate in responding. "I accept."

Kierian's head spins. Their next steps were always going to be set by Flora. Now they're becoming even clearer. She knows their names. They didn't leave the seelie court in peace. There seems to be no end to the dangers piling up around them. How they're supposed to take a stand against all of it, what they're able to do, is more than Kierian can think through without a little more time. Time they might not have.

"Let's prepare to depart as soon as we're able," Bayler says.

***

Vivian curls up on the couch next to her sister, the scent of soap coming from both of them. She leans into Cassie, the warmth of her keeping Vivian anchored in place. That and the lights of the apartment. Almost every word takes shape as a sound rather than a conversation. With her eyes closed, their voices give the darkness a shape that's not four damp walls.

There's something faint in her gut. It's not hunger, though it could be fear. But it feels alive, moving as if there's something just out of reach. She has no intention of reaching for it. Her whole world has been turned upside down, shaken, and set back down sideways. Even with her sister here next to her she can't get everything to feel right side up. She's not sure it ever will be again.

Then, that something inside her pulls. She gasps, the force of it nearly causing her to fall forward off the couch. Cassie catches her, holding her steady. Still, the force remains. It's drawing her forward. She can resist it, but everything in her starts to fall apart.

"Breathe, Viv, you have to breathe," Cassie says. Vivian's pulse speeds up and she repeats those words in her head. Breathe. In and out. Breathe. She has to keep breathing.

Hazel eyes come into her vision, vividly colored with bits of black streaming through the iris. It almost distracts Vivian from the feeling inside her, but it's too persistent.

"Hi," Flora says. She's crouched on the floor in front of her, looking up at Vivian. The sight of her is disarming.

"Hi." Vivian can hardly get the word out.

"Someone is looking for you," Flora says. The gentleness in her voice seems disconnected from her words. "Do you know who it might be?"

She's seen his face. She might not know his name, but she never wants to see him again. Vivian nods.

"You don't want them to find us, though?"

"No." Vivian's voice is stronger.

"They don't have to," Flora says. "They won't if you can let me help you. Can you do that?"

Vivian nods.

Flora places her palms face up in front of Vivian, but not touching her. "I need you to focus wholly on something else," Flora says. "You can take my hands, you can take your sister's, whatever will help you the best."

A shiver runs through Vivian, but she turns to her sister and holds out her hands. Cassie takes them without hesitation.

"Now, with everything you have, I need you to focus everything on her. Every thought, every breath, every sensation in your body."

Vivian squeezes her eyes shut and pulls her sister into a hug. Their knees bump and Vivian's side stretches painfully, but she holds her sister close. Let the whole world fall away, except for this, she thinks. And as heartbeats pass, without fully realizing it, the force within her fades.

"You're safe now," Cassie whispers. "I will do everything I can to protect you."

Her sister's words resonate through her. Vivian pulls back gently, taking a moment to look at Cassie's face. There's so much in the lines of her sister's face she's never seen before. It feels like so much time has passed so quickly, she almost doesn't recognize her, much less herself.

Vivian turns to Flora. "I can't feel it anymore," she says. There's a wonder in her voice she can't contain.

Flora nods. "As long as it holds, they can't find you," she says. "And even then, now you know how to stop them."

Vivian isn't quite sure, but there's something almost sad about the way Flora speaks. Vivian holds out a hand to Flora. She hesitates, glancing at Cassie, then puts her hand in Vivian's.

Vivian takes it, squeezing once. "Thank you, too."

Something passes over Flora in that moment. Vivian's emotions are too tired, battered, and beaten to imagine what it might be. Flora nods solemnly, then sits back in her chair.

Footsteps echo across the room and Vivian flinches. She curls into Cassie again, shutting her eyes. The only person who isn't with them is the only one she doesn't want to see. She knows his name. Cassie said he won't hurt her. Everything inside her mind and body can't believe that yet. He's not close to her, but even the same space causes her heartbeat to spike and her breathing to quicken.

Vivian squeezes Cassie's hand and pulls slightly, opening her eyes to catch her sister's gaze. Vivian moves her lips, no sound coming from her. "I need you." She doesn't have to say any more to get their longstanding safety message across. She needs to be alone with her sister.

"You said there was a separate bedroom?" Cassie says.

"Yes," Bayler says. "Down the hall to your left. No one has used it for a while, so it should be perfectly clean."

Cassie stands, gently coaxing Vivian up with her. Vivian still curls her shoulders in, using her sister as a shield and not letting go of her hand. "I think we're going to take a minute," Cassie says. "If you all don't mind."

"Is everything okay?"

A chill runs through Vivian.

"I think it will be," Cassie says.

As soon as the door is shut, Vivian can breathe again. She fills her lungs fully, holding her breath before letting it go. Cassie sits down on the bed and pats the space next to her.

"What's wrong?" Cassie says.

Vivian can feel her gaze but she's not sure how to answer. Even with a door and walls between them and the rest of the world, there's a pressure in her chest she can't let go of. A tension runs through her entire body. She's okay if they're alone, or if Flora and Bayler are with them. But something in her threatens to shatter every time she sees or hears him.

"Do you trust him?" Vivian says. There's a softness, something so incredibly fragile that stretches from her and into her words. She watches Cassie's mouth open, shut, then nod. Cassie pats the bed again, and this time Vivian sits down next to her. They turn to face each other, Cassie taking her hands.

"Who?" Cassie asks.

Vivian takes a shaky breath, changing her mind on what to say at the last moment. "Not Bayler."

"Kierian," Cassie says. Vivian shutters slightly at the name. "I do trust him."

Cassie reaches over, gently turning Vivian's face toward hers. "I found you," she says, her voice not leaving any room for doubt. "I always have, and I always will, continue to fight for you, Vivian. They hurt you. I don't know what happened and you don't ever have to tell me. I don't expect that to heal right away. None of us do. But I hope even if you can't quite believe it now, you know you don't have to be afraid. Not of him, not of anyone or anything else."

"Why do you keep calling me Viv?" It's all she can process at the moment. Everything else inside her is incapable of settling.

"It's a way to keep you safe," Cassie says. There's a strange sense of calm in her sister's voice, as if these are things she's known all her life. "Flora and Bayler are seelie fae. Similar to the fairy tales, but not quite. Using a nickname keeps you safer."

She frowns. "Their eyes are different colors," Vivian says. "Is that what you mean? That's how you can tell."

Cassie tilts her head slightly. "They look human otherwise?"

"Yes. Are they not supposed to?" There's a spike in Vivian's chest again.

"I'm not sure," Cassie says.

Vivian nods. There isn't an answer that will make this feel normal. None of this is normal. Still, her sister has answers that Vivian is floundering to discover. It's as if she's been shoved into a dark cave, but her guide left her without a light. At least Cassie has a light, even if it's him. Minutes and hours are too short a time to try and fix all the pieces that have fallen out of place. Vivian's not sure what the picture is supposed to be anymore. Who she is anymore.

"Can I have a few minutes?" Vivian says finally. "Just to think?"

"Are you sure that's what you need?" Cassie says.

Vivian nods. "Just... leave the door cracked open please."

Cassie hugs her sister. The warmth of the gesture soothes her. Vivian doesn't flinch. Then Cassie stands, the bed shifting to adjust to Vivian's weight. "I'll be right out here if you need me," Cassie says. Her sister crosses the room, pausing before swinging the door mostly closed.

"Thank you." Cassie can't hear her, but Vivian doesn't mind. Minutes are too short a time, but if everything up to this point has fractured minute by minute, maybe minute by minute she can at least let herself acknowledge that all the pieces are still hers.

Chapter 13

KIERIAN DOESN'T STOP PACING. His footsteps echo down the hallway, creating a rhythm that doesn't require him to think. He hears the door open. He catches Cassie's profile out of the corner of his eye as she steps into the hallway. Another glimpse of her leaning up against the wall. He can't bring himself to meet her eyes. She doesn't say a word.

Their bond stretches and wraps around him. It ripples slowly, a pressure building in his chest until finally it snaps. Kierian stops abruptly. Every single thought he's been reaching for suddenly converges. His fears come into focus and he's not entirely sure what to do with himself.

He lost something he can't ever get back. He never thought he'd ever worry whether or not being human was something that could be stolen from him until it was. He's been running from Cassie but also from himself. If he could put enough distance between the two of them, he could believe she wouldn't get hurt. He could pretend he isn't what he's been changed to be. His avoidance might have cost her life, the humanity of her sister, her own humanity.

It's at the conclusion of those thoughts that he turns toward her. She's still standing there, quietly watching. He wonders if she knows she's drawing his focus toward her. It's a faint sensation. It's more her presence than anything else, and Kierian can't quite understand why.

"I'm sorry, I didn't mean to distract you," Cassie says. She watches him intently, a slight frown on her face.

He shakes his head, taking a step toward her before hesitating. He can't quite tell the difference between their imprint and his own desire to be near her. "You didn't distract me," he says. More than that runs through his head, something like a "thank you for reaching out to me," or, "thank you for waiting," but he can't quite bring himself to say either of those things.

"Why are you out here?" she says. The question isn't meant to pierce him but it does. The pent-up thoughts and emotions inside him spill over, answering her questions and all the ones he's been asking himself.

"I could have been the reason you got hurt," Kierian says. "I could have been the reason you lost your sister, and it would have been my fault. I made a promise to myself as soon I realized what happened to me. When I understood what they turned me into. I never wanted anyone to imprint on me. If it put them in danger, if it meant they might end up turned, I didn't want to be a part of that. I know what they took from me. I didn't want to be the reason it happened to anyone else. I never wanted to take like that from anyone else."

"Kierian..."

"Please," he says. There's an ache in him that words can't fill, but only pouring them out can start to let that ache begin to mend. "Just give me a moment longer. What when on in that court, that's what I've been trying to fight. I never want to be like that. Bloodthirsty, drunk on power. I never wanted you to see me anywhere near that point.

When I dropped my guard, when you imprinted on me, it was the first moment I saw someone in danger and there was something I could do about it.

"You didn't ask for this. I didn't want this reality to be yours. I thought I could undo it, but I can't keep fighting out of grief or self-pity. I can't fight out of a fear of trying not to lose you, causing hurt to you directly or not. But I want to stay with you if you'll let me. Not just to fulfill a promise made to a fae, but because I have something I want to fight for. Not to try and fix a broken past, or atone for my mistakes..."

Kierian's words trail off. He watches her breathe, keeping his eyes on her face. The moments of quiet between them seems to go on so long he's tempted to break it himself. All he can do, though, is focus on the words he's said and on her presence. It's her answer he's waiting for, no matter what it is.

"You are here," Cassie says. Even just those words are more of a relief than he could ever imagine. "Despite everything, we are both here, I might have found you by accident before you meant for me too. I don't know what was happening in that court room, and I don't think I'll ever want to know. The thing is, no matter what promises you've made to yourself, you've kept every promise you made to me. What Vivian is going through is not your fault. I might not have found her if it wasn't for you. I lost my sister. You helped bring her back to me. I couldn't shield her from all the evil in the world any more than you can possibly shield me. It doesn't mean I'm going to stop trying. I think you're trying too. Can you live with that?"

He can't answer her question, though he desperately wishes he had the words. For the past year he's only seen faces with hunger and greed written on them. There's a gentleness in her expression and her words he's not quite sure how to accept.

"We could have been too late," Kierian says. They're the only words he can find. "We could have been too late and that still would have been my fault."

"Maybe," Cassie says. She doesn't hesitate but she also doesn't hide. "But she's here. We're safe, at least as safe as we can be. That's what matters now."

Kierian aches to be able to breathe again. That relief of pressure is denied to him. The space between them is too small and too wide at the same time.

"I may falter again, and I cannot promise that will be without consequence," Kierian says. "But I want to stay with you. I will continue to fight by your side if you'll let me." There's a vulnerability, a possibility of breaking. He can feel it in his bones, but he lets his words rest in the space between them.

Cassie bites her lip, a small smile forming. "I think I can do that." She opens her arms to each side, her eyes never leaving him.

At her invitation, he falls into her. He pulls her into a strong embrace. It's her hair, clean and slightly damp, that covers his shoulder. And the warmth of her body. He can feel the pull of her arms too, wrapped around him. There's the faintest scent of lavender. Miraculously, it drowns out even the memory of the smell of iron. In this moment, she's the only thing that exists to him.

***

"You seem to take this matter of bonds personally, more than I would expect from a fae," Bayler says quietly. Flora can hear him, but his voice doesn't carry down the hall to Vivian.

Flora's eyes scan his face before answering. "As someone who claims to have been a doctor, not taking bonds personally seems to be a lack of empathy for the patient."

Bayler tilts his head slightly. "I can separate intent and impact. You can reveal yourself on purpose with intent to do good and still cause a human harm. You can reveal yourself on purpose with intent to do harm and succeed or fail. Accidents can go either way."

"You would pardon the mythic completely?" Flora says. "Accidental or not, they still made a choice that revealed themselves."

Bayler's expression darkens, his jaw clenching then releasing. "I was a doctor, but I couldn't solve the root issue. Other imprints aren't something I can change. The damage was already done. I could only try and help each patient if they wanted to heal. Responsibility for intent lies with the mythic. The impact on the ones that imprinted on them is what I tried to help mend."

"If each bond a mythic makes is weaker than their last, how are they supposed to know the truth of what they can see?" Flora says.

"Only knowing a fraction of the truth isn't a mercy in itself?" Bayler says. "Even a mythic's first imprint can't see everything as they are. You don't believe that was designed with a purpose?"

Flora sighs. "I suppose you could argue that," she says. "But is it still a mercy if their imprint abandons them?"

Bayler leans back in the chair, watching Flora. There's a long moment of silence before he speaks again. "Yours meant something to you, didn't they?"

The knob of the front door clicks before either of them can speak. Flora's gaze snaps toward the door as Cassie and Kierian come back in. Bayler's eyes rest on Flora for just a beat longer before looking toward the pair as well.

"Are we interrupting something?" Kierian says.

Flora shakes her head. "I think we were just about done. There are more pressing things to consider than the past. We have to determine what comes next."

"It sounds like you have a plan," Kierian says.

"I do," Flora says. "I know how to get us into unseelie territory. Once we get in, we find evidence of their plans so we know what their next steps will be. We can use that evidence to undermine their plans. The best way to protect innocents is to prevent the unseelie from reaching them to begin with. We can't undermine them from within the court, but if we can get back outside, we can figure out our next steps."

Cassie only half listens as Flora speaks. Her gaze drifts toward the bedroom door. It's still slightly ajar but too narrow to see through. She made a promise to Flora, Kierian is by her side, but her love and loyalty to her sister runs deeper than either of those things.

"Go," Kierian says. Cassie jumps, convinced she's imagined him speaking until he says it again. "Go see her. We can wait." Flora nods toward the bedroom. It's all the permission Cassie needs.

"I'll be right back," she says. Cassie crosses to the bedroom, lightly pressing on the door. It swings in. She finds Vivian curled up on the edge of the bed, arms wrapped around her legs. She looks up to meet Cassie's eyes.

"Can I come in?" Cassie says.

Vivian nods.

Cassie crosses the room, sitting gently on the bed next to her. "You're still doing alright?" she asks.

Vivian nods again. "I think so."

Cassie takes a deep breath, putting one arm around her sister to hold her in an embrace. She can only imagine the thoughts running through her sister's head. Still, it's everything Cassie can do to stay grounded in this moment. She can imagine almost everything outside these four walls is normal. And following that imaginary reality is a question Cassie realized she's never let herself ask.

"Do you want to go home?"

Vivian breathes in sharply. Vivian's answer is hardly audible. Her lips move, but there's no audible answer at first.

"Yes," Vivian says finally. Before Cassie can speak, she continues. "I do, but I don't know what I'd do with myself. Nothing is the same anymore. Home wouldn't be the same, no matter how much I want it to be."

Cassie's heart aches. For as long as she's spent trying to shield her younger sister, there are only so many things she can fix, no matter what she wishes she could.

"We can still go home if you want," Cassie says. "We can make home ours again." Still, as the words leave her mouth, they sound hollow. They can't live like nothing has happened. She knows that, but she also can't take back her words.

Vivian takes another deep, shaky breath. "What do you want?"

Cassie blinks at the question. Thoughts tumble through her mind, a thousand possible answers falling flat. "What do I want?" Cassie says finally. "I want to help them. I want to stay with you and help them. I don't think I would have found you on my own, but I also can't lose you again."

Vivian nods. She gently extracts herself from Cassie's arms, pushing herself off the bed. Vivian takes a few steps toward the door before looking back. "Are you coming or staying here?" Vivian says. The faint smile at the edge of Vivian's mouth, a shadow of the sister that she knew before, stirs Cassie's heart.

"I'm coming."

The two of them make their way back into the living room. Kierian meets Cassie's eyes for only a moment before darting away. Neither fae takes their eyes off them.

Vivian's hands curl into fists at her side. She looks up from the ground, making eye contact with Flora. "You're fighting for people like me, right? Who have seen things they weren't supposed to, without any help?" she says. Her voice is small, but it doesn't waver.

Flora nods. "People aren't things to be spirited away and then abandoned. You shouldn't be alone in trying to understand this new layer of the world. But I didn't get a chance..."

"I heard you talking from the other room, even though you were trying to whisper," Vivian says. "I want to help. I want to stay."

Cassie squeezes her sister's hand once, the ache in her heart too strong to simply let exist without doing anything. "Are you sure?" Cassie asks. Facing whatever lies ahead is a burden, one Cassie isn't sure she can carry much less watch her sister wrestle with. But there's a driven curiosity that, despite everything, hasn't been stolen from Vivian yet.

Vivian nods. "I have to do something. Trying to pretend will only make it worse, I think."

Flora smiles faintly. "You remind me of someone I used to know," she says. There's something bittersweet in her voice, but Cassie doesn't have time to ask before she moves on, the smile disappearing. "We're in this together, then. Let's gather what we need and get going. We don't need to give anyone else a chance to stop us. Whatever happens, we go together."

"We go together," Vivian whispers.

Cassie's certain there's not enough space in her heart to contain the love she has for her sister, especially having almost lost her.

"Always," Cassie says. "We always go together."

Chapter 14

FLORA AND BAYLER TAKE the lead through the city streets. Cassie and Vivian stay close to them while Kierian follows behind. As the sun dips ever closer to the horizon, most of those passing by on the streets are too preoccupied to take any notice of them. The street gives them anonymity Kierian wishes could last longer.

They turn down a street Kierian doesn't recognize and that's when his fantasy is shattered. Flora stops suddenly halfway through a brick alley. Bayler steps quickly in front of her and Kirian mirrors his movement. He closes the distance between him and the two sisters. He glances over his shoulder, scanning the area for anything unusual. He can't see or hear what put Bayler on edge, but that doesn't mean a threat isn't present.

"I don't think we're alone," Bayler says.

"We're probably not," Flora says. Then, raising her voice, "If you've been biding your time looking for me, you've been successful. You found me. If you have something to say you can come out now."

There's a clatter down the street ahead of them, around a corner. Still, nothing visible to Kierian moves.

"If you're trying to stop me, though, that's a mistake," Flora says. They start walking again, Flora stepping ahead of Bayler. They're met with silence.

They make it a little bit further through the city, the sun beginning to set, and the clouds illuminated with muddy colors. They turn down another small street, hardly wide enough for them to walk in pairs. The sky above the tops of the buildings shifts to a haunting shade of orange. The hue taints everything it touches, only heightening the tension in the air. Pink clouds bleed into cherry-tinged rays of light.

"You have a long life yet ahead of you, Flora. You can still come home."

The prince's voice echoes down the alley. Streetlights flicker, casting a sickly glow onto the cobblestone. Flora's hands tighten into fists, her bone-like armor jutting out of her skin appearing slightly more hazel.

"Are you going to show yourself? There's no reason to hide if you only want to talk, is there?" Flora says.

In front of them, the seelie prince steps into the center of the alley. The motion doesn't hide the sound of footsteps echoing behind them. Kierian's gaze darts back to find a group of four other seelie fae. They're surrounded. Not outnumbered, but this is all the fae Kierian can see. There could be more hiding in shadows or around a corner.

"I'm offering you one last chance to turn back," the prince says.

"Turn back from what?" Flora says. "I'm afraid I don't understand what you mean."

The prince holds out his hands to either side of him, empty palms facing them. "Turn back from abandoning your home, your people, your position. There is still a place for you in my court and by my side. But like I said when you left, this is the last chance I can offer you."

Flora's voice shakes. "I walked away already," she says. "I lost my home, my place, and my people the moment I stepped past that sector line. You offer me something that you cannot restore, no matter what you promise me. My trust in your court has been broken for a long time. That wound has not healed. No second chance, no third chance, can mend that. That bridge has long been destroyed.

"You killed my imprint. I know you will never say it, but I know his blood is on your hands. If not by your hands, by a command that you gave. I didn't choose my place by your side. You demanded it of me, and I was expected to fill it, thankful for the help in ridding me of all other distractions. You say you offer me one last chance to come home? That is not a home you can tempt me to return to."

Time seems to lengthen, falling sideways like the light of the sunset. Finally, the prince speaks. "Then I hold you no longer captive," he says. "Whether the home you leave behind is full or empty, clean or blood soaked, I set you free of it. If those are the words you've longed to hear, I will give you that much. You are free of the seelie court. But you also may no longer find a place in my land, not even for refuge. That is the choice you have made. I don't claim full innocence in any matter, you know that, but I would not be so quick as to assign guilt either."

"I've witnessed all I need to," Flora says. "Whether you admit the truth or not, I know."

"And you alone can determine what is right and wrong?" the prince says.

Bayler speaks softly, though his words echo in the alley. "I think it's time for us to go." He places a hand on Flora's shoulder, gently pushing her forward. "I believe this is where the conversation ends. He's granted you leave. Take it."

"Goodbye, Flora," the prince says. He steps to the side, but the size of the alley forces each of them to pass by him in a single file line. No one looks back. There's nothing for any of them to gain.

The five of them continue, the street widening and narrowing again. The sky darkens, and Flora's pace falters. Cassie walks faster to try and reach her, but the fae is already dropping herself to the ground by the time Cassie is at her side.

"Flora, what's wrong?" Cassie says.

Flora shakes her head, lowering her face to her hands. "You don't understand," she says. "I've been fighting for so, so long. But every step of the way I've never gotten far enough. It never seems far enough."

Cassie looks up as Bayler crouches next to them. "I know," he says. "But the length of time in which we get to fight is a blessing and a curse. It's the cause, and the hope of the resolution, that drives one forward."

Flora breaths shakily. "He's the only thing I know how to fight for," she says. She catches her breath between tears. "I couldn't keep him safe. I couldn't protect what meant the world to me. It's important that no one else ever has to know what that's like, that the mythic and the human are protected, but I don't know how to keep going when he's been gone so long. All I ever seem to do is lose something more."

Bayler puts one hand on Flora's shoulder. "You are not alone anymore," he says.

"And the rest of it?" Flora says, her voice a whisper. "Everything that's lost, and everything that could be?"

"We don't know," Kierian says. He speaks gently, setting a hand on Cassie's back as he crouches beside her. "We can't know the things you've lost, your fight, and the obstacles you've faced to get here. But you're not alone anymore. You also don't have to keep pushing along this path as the only way to remember him. This can't save the past, but we haven't lost the future yet."

At first his words seem to help, but by the end she's crying again, curled tighter in on herself. A yellow lightbulb casts a long shadow on her. Kierian looks to Cassie for help. Her lips are slightly parted, but she seems stuck in place.

Vivian speaks through the crying. Flora doesn't respond, so she repeats herself, raising her voice slightly. "What was his name?"

Flora looks up finally, taking a deep breath. "Jayce." Her voice cracks as she speaks.

"What do you remember most about him?" Vivian says. She still stands apart from the rest of them, her hands crossed over her stomach, but she watches Flora intently.

Flora breathes deeply and wipes away her tears. She stays curled up, but she does answer. "He was curious," Flora says. "He wanted to know everything about the world I could see. He was scared at first too, like everyone is I imagine, but he didn't let it scare him for long. The genuine curiosity, a sweet and gentle desire to discover the world around him, was always there. It was the first time in a long time I was ever really seen for who I was, not what someone wanted me to be."

A grimace washes over Flora's features, but she doesn't start crying again. When she looks up, Vivian is still watching her. "I wish we could have met him," Vivian says.

"I wish he was here," Flora says.

"Is there anything we can do?" Vivian says.

Flora draws herself up to standing, using the wall as a guide. She meets each of their eyes individually, settling on Vivian last. "Stay with me," Flora says. "Thank you, each of you. But we have to keep going. Not out of obligation, but in the hopes of something better."

Kieran nods. "I can stand for that."

***

Flora leads the group with renewed confidence. Her steps don't waver. Each street she takes with the precision of someone who's come this way many times before. The architecture of the city changes subtly as they walk, slowly revealing to them they're approaching another district.

Cassie leans toward her sister. "It's pretty, isn't it? The cement between the bricks seems to have veins running through them, like they're glowing."

Vivian studies the walls they pass by, frowning as she traces the walls with her eyes. She tries to make the colors appear but all she sees is standard brick and mortar. There's nothing unique about them. Carvings in the brick make a decorative pattern, but they don't have any strange coloring to them. They're just bricks and cement.

Before she can answer, Flora speaks, saving her from having to answer. "I've found it. There shouldn't be any traffic through here but stay alert and be careful."

Vivian is immediately drawn to the beauty of the archway Flora leads them toward. It's made of stone, though it doesn't lead any-where. It's walled up with bricks. But these bricks aren't standard. Their colors seem to shift, engravings of all different styles creating a dissonant mural. A few of the engravings are in completely different styles or colors. A few of them seem newer, as if this place has been repaired over the years.

There's something about it that draws Vivian in. It could be the vines and flowers carved into the arch, it could be something else entirely. She's not entirely sure, but at this moment, curiosity overcomes the fear. Vivian only realizes she's taken a few steps toward it when Flora claps a hand on her shoulder. She jumps, and Flora quickly lets go.

"I have to open it first and hold it open for the rest of you," Flora says. "This was built by unseelie hands. Even if you managed to get through, you wouldn't be able to get out on your own."

Flora steps forward, running a hand along the arch. She traces the designs, pushing pieces in with a practiced hand. "There's a mental fortification built into it," Flora says, explaining as she works. "Without proper permissions it's impossible for any non-fae to open. I might not be completely authorized but I think I can get it open. It should remember me. This should let me hold it open long enough for the rest of you to pass through."

Flora presses a final block into the wall. The entire carved line of writhing vines is pressed back into the stone, framing the arch. "As soon as I'm underneath it, I need each of you to pass through it as fast as you can. Okay?" Flora says. She doesn't wait for a reply.

Flora whispers words Vivian can't make out. She stands taller, pushing her arm then half her body underneath the arch. Her body shifts through it. Vivian stares with wide eyes as half of Flora disappears, stepping underneath the arch. What appeared to be a solid brick wall seems to swallow Flora up. Bayler starts moving, drawing her attention as Flora's hands begin to shake.

"Quickly," Bayler says. He goes first. The brick backing to the arch appears to be no barrier for him. Cassie passes through, and Vivian's stomach turns over watching her sister disappear. There's no pain as Vivian puts an arm through. She steps through it, bracing herself for what might be on the other side. Relief floods her as she finds Cassie and Bayler standing there, a metal tunnel stretching out behind them. Kierian passes through last, reaching out a hand for Flora as he gets to the other side.

"She has to be the one to let go," Bayler says. His words are even, but there's a frown as he speaks.

Flora bows her head, hands still pressed firmly against the arch. She takes one more gasping breath before she leans toward the four of them. She flinches as she pulls her hands back. Bayler is already there to help pull her to their side of the arch.

Flora's breaths are shallow. Her eyes pass over each one of them, her lips moving. As soon as she mouths "four," she leans heavily against the side of the passage, letting Bayler help keep her on her feet.

"We're about halfway there now," Flora says, taking a deep breath. "We only have one more door to pass through before we're in the heart of Unseelie territory. Then the real fun begins."

***

For all Kierian's vague familiarity with the fae, the changes in the tunnel still awe him. The veins of the wall grow in complexity as the material shifts from brick to metal plating. Color emanates from every surface like glowing fissures, fireworks preserved on the metal's surface. He's not totally convinced the patterns are static. If they have a purpose, which is likely, Kierian can't decipher what they might mean.

Flora steps quietly around a bend in the tunnel. She holds out a hand behind her and the rest of them pause. Kierian narrows his eyes, but he can't see around the bend. Flora's voice makes him jump.

"Servin?"

"Flora?" a voice says. "Flora, it is you! Why are you here? You would have had to fight the barrier. What madness possessed you to do that?"

"It's good to see you too," Flora says. She speaks as if he's a friend, but the softness of her tone fades. "I didn't come all this way for a visit. You know that as well as I do."

Flora motions to them, and the four come around the bend. Kierian makes it just in time to see the unseelie fae's features fall into a frown. The sharp lines of his face cause his bones to look as if they're ready to jump clean out of him, the blood in his veins a deep, writhing green. The structure of his jaw and the scaled natural armor are similarly structured but angled differently than Flora's. Only subtle differences divide them.

"Look at me," Flora says. Her tone is even but her voice commands attention. "Servin, look at me. These are my friends. You can trust me, so you can trust them."

Servin doesn't relax but he doesn't make any sudden moves. Kierian watches him closely. The tunnel continues as far as he can see, but there's only a short sprint's distance between where they stand and the door Servin guards. There's a panel next to the door, two pipes running up and into the ceiling. Somehow that must control how it works.

"I trust you, Flora," Servin says. "But you know the terms I'm bound to."

"I know," Flora says. "But I need you to listen to me. Are you really on board with everything they're planning to do? Breaking the accords, starting a war, weaponizing innocents? I wouldn't think that would sit well with you."

Servin takes one step back toward the door, one hand reaching for his waist. Kierian can't see past his cloak but he can imagine what he might be reaching for. "I need you and your friends to leave," Servin says. "Otherwise, I will sound the alarm."

"Listen to me first," Flora says. Her hands begin to shake before she presses them to her sides. "You know what they're planning to do, don't you? The mass revelation of mythics to the humans. That is why I'm here, Servin."

Servin frowns, taking another step back. "It doesn't matter what I think," he says. "My duty is to do what I'm told. Your court should know better than to get involved with this." There's an edge to his voice now. His tone sets Kierian on edge too. Kierian glances over at Bayler, meeting the other fae's gaze.

"They do," Flora says, her voice rising. "That's why I'm here without their parade of status and importance. They wouldn't listen to me. I wasn't going to pretend nothing was wrong, waiting for everything to fall apart to do something, so they cut me off. I'm not here for anyone else. Maybe I should know better too, but here I am."

Kierian tests the unseelie's focus, taking one step forward. Servin's gaze darts directly toward him. Kierian heeds the stern glare sent his way. If they're going to stand a chance at getting past Servin, they need to be close enough to stop him before the fae can pull the alarm.

"You could stay here," Servin says. "A fae's life without a court only means you'll start to wither away until there's nothing left of you. It's a sentence of loneliness." There's a genuine softness to his words.

"I think you underestimate a fae's capacity for loneliness," Bayler says, jumping in. "And what it can drive one to."

Flora glances back at Kierian and Bayler. Her glare sends a very clear message: stay back. Flora's footsteps alone echo down the corridor as she approaches Servin, her pace even and her voice never breaking.

"You've offered me a place here," she says. Her words seem to linger in the air, heavier than the echo of them. She stops in front of Servin. He's taller than she is, but Kierian can see what the unseelie fae can't - Flora reaches for her pistol as she speaks. "It's a generous offer. One I appreciate. As old friends, it's something I couldn't ask for, but you've offered anyway. As for my answer..."

Once Flora starts moving, Kierian jumps in front of Cassie and Vivian, trying to shield them. He stretches out his arms, turning his back to the scene. He squeezes his eyes shut and waits for an ear-splitting sound. It never comes. There's a hard thud, followed by another hard thud. Cassie sets a hand on his arm, peering over him.

"She hit him with the grip," Cassie says. Kierian looks over his shoulder. Sure enough, Servin lies slumped on the ground. Flora holsters the gun again, no blood anywhere to be seen.

Bayler is the first one to reach Flora's side. "He won't be out for long," Bayler says. "Let's get this door open." He starts to reach for the door, but Flora stops him.

"Don't," she says. "We're going to need my old friend one more time."

Bayler raises his eyebrows. "As in?"

"He's the only one who can open it without setting off the alarm."

"Leave that to me." Bayler picks the unseelie off the floor, propping up Servin with his own body. Bayler's breaths are even, but the longer he holds the fae up the more rugged his breathing gets. Flora takes Servin's hand and holds it to a panel in the wall.

A wheel, concealed in shadow behind an outcropping of stone, starts spinning rapidly. Bayler lets the fae down as gently as he can, though Servin's body still thuds against the ground. Flora pushes the door open with her boot as Kierian and the two sisters come forward.

"They'll be expecting us soon enough," Bayler says.

Flora smiles grimly. "We'll have to get what we came for before they find us then, won't we?"

Chapter 15

Passing through the tunnel door, Vivian can almost believe she's stepped into something magical. It doesn't look like the same city. Dark cloths hang between the tops of buildings, creating the illusion that every street is a covered walkway. The filtered sunlight casts a haze over her skin. The windows are draped with cloth too. It's as if every surface is a shadow.

It's a darkness that's alive. It shimmers with fibers of different colors. The shadows have a hint of starlight in them, light refracting into different points of light and rainbows. There could be whole galaxies caught up in these dark places and Vivian would never know. She doesn't doubt it's possible. Everything up to this point has been a blur. There's been a darkness clouding every experience, every drop of blood, every flash of fangs, and the soreness in every muscle. But this... She never could have dreamed of this.

There's a slight tug at her arm. "We can't stop," Flora says. "I know it's a sight. It always is, the first and the hundredth time you see it, but there's danger in it too. We can't let it captivate us. This whole place is like a spider's web. If you get stuck in it, there's no way out."

Vivian takes Cassie's hand and stays by her side. Flora walks through the streets like she knows where she's going, at least that's how it looks to Vivian. She's unfazed by corners and doesn't hesitate at any intersection. There's a silence in this sector of the city. If there's anyone else around, Vivian can't see them.

It's not until they reach a sprawling building that Vivian sees any hint of life. A tall decorative gate leads into a green square, enclosed by a wrought iron fence. It's a brooding building. Spires and towers peek beyond the cloth ceiling and into the true sky. Warm light glows from the windows. Walking along the inside perimeter of the gate are two guards. Vivian frowns as she watches them, but her eyes aren't strong enough to make out any details about them in the dim light.

"They've gathered their court again," Bayler says. Even as a whisper, his voice seems to shatter the stillness around them.

"With no representative envoy from the seelie," Flora says. There's enough venom in those words to make Vivian cringe. "If they're going to enact their plan, they have to do it now. The next time they break the accords there will be repercussions."

At that moment, a single pitch rings through the city. It's so high Vivian almost can't hear it. Bayler cringes, squeezing his eyes shut and taking a step back. Flora winces.

"That's the alarm," Flora says. "We go now."

The large gate in front of the towering meeting place starts to open. Fae begin to pour out down the steps of the central building, making their way into the streets. Vivian's breath catches in her throat, her chest tightening. Even hidden in the shadows doesn't mean they won't be found. But Flora doesn't stand still or head back the way they came. She darts down a side street, directing the rest of them silently. Vivian holds tightly to her sister's hand.

Flora angles to the right of the main gate, staying in the shadows as they follow the perimeter fence. Vivian watches the fae exit the main gate to their left. As far as she can tell, no one wanders or stays behind in the courtyard. Flora stops at a small gate set into the fence. It's much less decorative, only tall enough for an average size being to pass through. Flora steps out into the open as she approaches it. There is no shouting, no pointing, hardly any extra sound at all. No guard stands watch. Still, Flora makes no move to open it.

A curiosity fills Vivian. She takes a step forward. Flora watches her, though the silence stays unbroken between them. Vivian puts out her hand, as if to push open the gate. Flora nods. Oddly enough, a smile starts to form as Vivian takes hold of the gate and pushes it open. There's no tingling sensation, no pain like she imagined Flora felt trying to get them in here. It's just a regular iron gate.

Flora mouths the words "thank you," and passes through the small gate into the courtyard. There's no one left to pay the five of them any attention. Still, Flora stays close to the fence, following it until they reach the edge of the building. The only way in Vivian can see is through the front doors. They're decorative, inset with stained glass and silver handles. As they get closer, Vivian can see light spilling out between them. They're not shut. Flora pulls the doors open just enough for them to slip through.

They step into an expansive room with a raised ceiling and detailed tiling. Their footsteps echo, bouncing back to them. Vivian's heartbeat feels loud to her ears, but there's no echo of that at least. There's a grand staircase offset to one side, hallways splitting off on the left and right. Directly ahead of them is another room. There's no door, but an intricate wrought iron gate is closed over the entrance.

Flora moves toward the gate. The room past it has lights strung along the top of the walls and down the rows of chairs. The circular room contains different levels of seating, all lowering down into a central arena of sorts with a pedestal at its center.

"If they left any trace of what they were up to before the alarm went off, it will be in here. This is where their court meets," Flora says in a whisper. She reaches a hand out as if to trace the patterns on the gate, but she never touches the metal.

"I can open it," Vivian says. No one has asked anything of her, but if she was able to get through the first gate, it would stand to reason she should be able to open this one too.

Flora steps back. "Thank you," she says.

This gate isn't locked either. Vivian takes the left side, swinging it wide until it rests against the wall. She does the same to the other side, fully clearing the entrance into the room. The hinges don't make a sound. The smallest bit of pride starts to grow in Vivian's heart. She might be starting to make a difference.

***

The gathering place of the Unseelie feels like an inverted version of the vampire clan's. The speaker here would be below everyone, their attention focused down rather than on someone standing above them. Each chair here appears to be carved out of stone. The etchings are worn, though, as if they've been used for many years.

Cassie steps inside the room, falling behind Kierian and Bayler. Flora descends the steps down to the center of the room. Bayler splits off to one side, staying on the top few levels of the amphitheater-style chamber. Cassie stays close to her sister. Still, she can't resist the pull of the place. She wanders down the steps and through a row of seats. Kierian paces one row above the bottom floor.

It's Bayler's whispered mutterings that draw Cassie's attention. She pauses, Vivian stopping behind her. She looks up to see Bayler standing from a crouching position. That's when she starts to hear the rumbling; that's when she sees stone doors starting to cover the entrance.

"Run!"

Cassie propels her sister forward ahead of her, trying to get the both of them back to the stairs. Out of the corner of her eye, Cassie sees Kierian pike over the last row of seats, landing on the bottom floor of the room just as Vivian and Cassie reach the stairs leading up to the exit. Her sister ahead of her, Cassie spares one glance back.

"Keep going. I'm right behind you," Kierian says.

Bayler is on the other side of the closing door. Flora follows closely behind. She reaches out for Vivian's hand, pulling her through the half-way covered entrance. Cassie reaches out too, just a few steps behind.

Cassie's foot catches on the very last step. The sudden shift in balance sends her sprawling. Her hands hit the ground hard, pain spiking through her palms and wrists. Kierian is there, his hands pulling her to her feet. As she looks up, Flora holds Vivian back from running through the narrow sliver of space between the wall and stone.

Kierian pulls Cassie forward. She manages to keep her balance but she's not fast enough. The stone doors shut, separating her from her sister and dividing the rest of them.

"Cassie!" Her sister's voice is faint through the stone.

"Viv!" Cassie squeezes her eyes shut, hitting the stone once with an open palm. She hisses at the pain of impact. Cassie leans her forehead against the stone, laying a hand on it instead of hitting it again. She closes her eyes, willing the stone to move.

"Is there a lever? A brick, anything?" Flora's voice.

There's a brief shuffling near Cassie. "If there is I can't find anything," Kierian says. "I don't think I can get this open from our side."

"I can't pry it open," Flora says. "I don't know what triggers it and we don't have time to test it from this side. Stay put, stay out of sight, and we'll come back for you once we've found what we need."

"No!" Vivian's voice is high, louder than Flora's. "I won't leave her."

"Stay with Flora," Cassie says. Her heart aches, but she has to trust Flora is right. "We'll be okay. We came here for a reason and we've got to finish this. When you're done we'll be here waiting. The door might open on its own by then, but we will be here waiting for you."

"You know you can't keep that promise," Vivian says.

Cassie can imagine her sister's face, disheveled and wide-eyed. She can never quite prepare herself for the memory of seeing a fragile girl running out of that dark place in the vampire enclave. That's the face she imagines on the other side of the door: her sister that she can't reach.

"I can't get this door open," Cassie says. "That's all I know for certain, but we're not giving up. Please, go. You'll be safe with them until I'm with you again."

"We're coming back for you," Vivian says.

Cassie nods once, the stone scraping her forehead lightly. "I know you will," Cassie says. "I know. We'll find each other again. We always have."

***

It takes everything and more out of Vivian to step away from the stone door separating her from her sister. She clenches her jaw, her hands in fists. She can hear one of the fae take a few steps back, but just as Vivian turns toward them her world tilts violently sideways.

Vivian gasps, clutching at her stomach with both hands. "I can feel him again," she says. The words come out between gasps. "He's trying to find me. I-"

It's Flora's hands on her shoulders that shock her. Vivian jumps, her walls coming up as she curls in on herself. "Don't touch me." There's no malice in the words, but she means them. Her voice almost breaks. But her body shivers; it remembers.

"They're coming back," Flora says. She crouches on the floor, taking up most of Vivian's vision. "We need to move fast."

"Out," Vivian says. She whispers the words as she imagines his half-blurred face she's only seen in shadows and never wants to see in the light. "Out, out, out, out, out!" With one final gasp the violent tugging leaves her. There's an emptiness in its place but she can breathe again.

"Okay," Vivian says. She pulls herself to her feet, a bit wobbly, but Flora helps steady her. "I can go."

Flora hesitates. Vivian takes a few steps away, standing on her own. With that, Flora nods and starts down the hallway. She looks back occasionally, but Vivian never meets her eyes. Every nerve in her body screams at her to go back but she pushes herself forward. Her sister has to be right. They'll come back, and she'll still be there when they do.

Vivian quickly loses track of the twisting and turning hallways. She couldn't find her way back alone even if she wanted to. They walk in a suffocating silence. The lights seem to get dimmer the further they go. One particularly dark hallway has walls made of stone, the only source of light coming from sparsely lit torches along the wall. At the end of the hallway, soft light trickles from underneath a closed door. They walk the length of that long, barred hallway, stopping at the very end.

"That has to be it," Flora says. Her whisper feels like a shout. Vivian's not sure if the echo of her voice is from the small corridor or inside her head. A chill digs into her body, clinging to her bones. She keeps her eyes trained on the floor or the wall to her left. If she looks right, she'll see iron bars with locks and filled with shadows. The sooner she can get away from here and back to her sister, the better.

Vivian can only see the vague outline of Flora moving from one side of a wooden door to the other. There's a faint click, and light floods out of the room as the door opens. Vivian squints, her eyes so used to the dark she's blinded for a moment. There's a figure standing out against the light. He's backlit, the lines of his face cast in shadow, but Vivian is drawn to his eyes.

A deep violet gaze sweeps over her. Deep pockets underneath his eyes catch even more shadow. The bones along his face don't look natural. They're in the wrong spots. His nose seems small, almost set into his face, cheekbones slightly lower than they should be, and a jawbone that's angled at the chin. Blue-violet veins, darkest at the outside corner of his eyes, run across his face and down his neck.

"Flora," he says. "I regret that I couldn't greet you with a warmer welcome. I hope you can pardon the lack of formalities present. Still, it's a pleasure to see you again. What is the reason that you've graced my court with your presence?"

"You know," Flora says. Her voice is unsteady. "You left me no choice. I couldn't stand by and watch with the burden of knowing what was to come. Your people may have turned me out, but I still know what lies ahead. I could not stand by and let it happen." Flora's hands begin to shake.

"There's always a choice," he says. "As you said, it's your own actions that have led you here today. That was my hope, but it's never a guarantee when you leave things up to an individual. You were always one for rules and peace. When those things are disturbed, you can't leave them be, can you?"

"This is your realm," Flora says. "If you wanted me here you had the power to make it happen. I know breaking rules and peace are a pastime of yours, but you're right. I will not let those things be warped. Whatever it is you want from the seelie court, whatever it is you want from me, you can speak plainly. What is it you cannot do within the bounds of the fae accords? Why wait for me?"

He smiles, the incisors just a little too sharp, even if he is a fae. "I am the king of this court. I can take whatever it is that I want, but it is much more satisfying when it comes into my hands by means other than by force. I wanted you to walk into this place willingly and here you are."

Footsteps echo behind them. Vivian's attention darts toward the sound. A sea of unseelie fae coming toward them down the hall. Bayler moves closer to her, positioning himself between her and the crowd.

When she turns back, she finds Flora with her hands no longer at her side but held out in front of her with the pistol aimed at the king. He's still smiling.

"I ask again, what is it you want from me?" Flora says. "Please. I'm interested to hear your request so I can give us both the pleasure of declining."

"You conduct yourself in court with much more grace, Flora," the king says. "You'd do well to regain that poise. But this isn't a simple exchange. You must've known that when you dared to step foot here without our consent. You'll find out what it we want from you, but that time has not yet come."

Hands grab Vivian. One closes over her mouth, stifling a scream before it can escape as she's jerked backward. Bayler meets the same fate.

A loud crack splits the air. Vivian's ears ring, a high-pitched static the only thing she can hear. She squeezes her eyes shut as she fights against the arms holding her. Her feet lift off the ground and panic rises in her chest as her motion is constrained.

Through the static, she begins to hear words again. "Patience, Flora. I truly did expect better of you, though I suppose you'll get a second chance. Not all of us can live up to the expectations others hold of us," the king says. "Keep them here. We'll call on them when they're ready."

Vivian is carried down the hall rather than walking. Every sound, every pinprick of sensation seems to press in on her, suffocating. She only opens her eyes again when her feet hit the ground, staring at a cell.

The bars squeal in protest as the door is opened, and she can't keep herself from trembling anymore. They let go of her, and with a push she stumbles forward. The door locks and Vivian's knees collapse under her. Flora catches her before she hits the ground. There's not a gun in her hands or at her waist anymore.

"I missed," Flora whispers, letting Vivian go. She stares down at her hands, open in front of her. They're still pale. Vivian recoils once she realizes why the thought matters. She's looking for blood on the fae's hands too. There's none, but just the act makes her stomach clench.

"We're not going back for them, are we?" Vivian asks the question even though she knows the answer. She is trapped, there's nowhere to go, and her sister is not here. Darkness wraps itself around her. Neither Flora or Bayler say a word, and silence stretches over them. Vivian's thoughts spiral as her tears come.

Chapter 16

"What do we do now?" Cassie says, her voice wavering. It's the same question Kierian has been asking himself since the door closed on them.

"We're not getting out that way so we might as well look for another way out," Kierian says. "There has to be one." The suggestion sounds hollow to his own ears, but he's not sure what else to offer her in support. Without knowing why the door closed, opening it is a nearly impossible task.

Kierian walks along the top row, one palm pressed against the outer wall. "Anything," he says. "Please let there be something." The words aren't meant for anyone but himself, a plea to the unknown. Still, he can hear Cassie's quite echo of his words across the room.

"Anything, please."

There's nothing he can find. None of the stones give way, none of the decorations do anything, and there are no doors he can find. Not even the place Bayler was when all this started gives him a clue. Kierian leans back, letting Cassie pass him. He closes his eyes, listening. It's the only thing left he can think of. The only sound he should hear is Cassie's footsteps, but there's something else.

"Cass, stand still for a minute."

"Why?"

Kierian doesn't answer. He's focused on the distant sounds from beyond the stone wall. Where before there was mostly silence, noise outside is getting louder. They must be coming back.

"We need to find a place to hide," Kierian says. "Now."

This time Cassie doesn't question him. Along the top row of the room, right by the entrance, is a countertop surface. The bottom of it is hollowed out, a curtain covering the space underneath. It doesn't reach quite the floor, but if everyone is coming and going at once it might give them all the cover they need.

"Here," Kierian says. He pulls back the curtain, letting Cassie squeeze into the space first. Kierian positions himself the best he can between Cassie and the curtain. If someone finds them before they can escape, they'll have to go through him first. Cassie breathes softly, her heart beating rapidly. For a minute or two, everything is quiet. Then, a deep rumbling sound begins as the stone door opens.

The room fills. Kierian can see shadows and shoes as the unseelie file back into their court. He holds himself as still as possible. He catches snippets of conversation around them, but Kierian keeps his layout of the room in his head. Unless they closed silently, the doors should still be open. Still, he can't see from this angle. The nerves in his body are urging him to run. If can just hold out a little longer, once no one is here, they might be able to slip out completely unnoticed. If they go now, they'll have to run. Kierian has no way of knowing how far they'll be able to get on their own.

A sudden silence falls over the room. "Let this court return to order," a voice says, his words cutting through the stillness. "We know what lies ahead. Some of us have already received our orders, beginning to carry them out. Some of us will in time. But let this moment be a reminder to you that no plan is ever perfected. It is each surprise that sharpens us, and our reactions we must control in order to conduct ourselves as we desire. We know what the end purpose we seek is, though, don't we? So let us fight for our ruling right, as the court of the fae. As the ruling court of both worlds, mystic and mundane."

A roar runs through the crowd. Kierian grits his teeth. None of them know what it's like to grow up human. None of them know what it's like to not have a choice in seeing this new world, or to become a part of it. But they're not chasing after knowledge. There's no thought of the consequences, for them or for anyone else. All they're focused on is power.

Kierian shifts slightly. He tenses, but there's nothing he can do to stop the curtain from rustling. The fae continues speaking. For a moment Kierian lets himself hope that no one heard it. He sees shoes just before the curtain is pulled sharply away, an unseelie fae looming over him.

Without ceremony, Kierian and Cassie are dragged to the front of the council. Kierian has more than enough things he'd like to say, but he keeps them to himself. He's positioned in front of the podium, Cassie beside him. She reaches for his hand, and he takes it quickly.

"For what purpose have you come here?" the unseelie fae says. There's a deep orange to his veins, a coloring Kierian hasn't seen before.

"Our own." Kierian answers with no hesitation.

"And what does your... friend say?" He turns his gaze to Cassie. She takes a step back. Kierian holds on to her firmly. He has words on his tongue, but she speaks before he can draw the fae's attention back to himself.

"We were curious," she says. Her voice wavers and the fae smiles.

He takes a step around the podium toward Cassie. Kierian steps between them, earning hard glares from those around him in the first row. "Don't touch her," Kierian says.

The fae stops just a foot away, looming over both of them, at least a foot taller than Kierian. "Curious about what?" he says. "And believe me, the power is in truth. A lie won't get you anywhere here."

Cassie's voice is a whisper. "To stop your plan."

"And what plan would that be?"

"A mass revelation," Cassie says. Kierian stares at the fae, watching him for any movement toward Cassie. He holds steady. Kierian forces himself to stay still too.

"And how do you suppose we're going to do that?"

"I don't know."

Kierian flexes his hands. The fae glances at him and backs up a few steps. "Satisfactory," the fae says. Then he turns to address the crowd. "You've heard their statements. My judgment is only in the stead of our king's presence. Shall we detain them until a course of action can be ascertained?"

The room fills with polite clapping. Kierian frowns. Nothing about this procession cheers him. It's all a show. Still, it must be a show of approval, as the fae holding each of them start to move, propelling them toward the stairs. Kierian loses his grip on Cassie, the fae separating them. Kierian can feel her heartbeat along their bond. As long as she doesn't get any further from him, he can hold himself together. The moment she's in danger he will not hesitate.

***

After a dizzying series of hallways, stairs, and corners, Cassie and Kierian are deposited in a mostly barren room. The only door is the one they came in, and two windows on the far side are covered with plywood and nailed shut. Even the air seems shut in, a musty scent reaching Cassie's nose.

The door shuts and locks behind them and the room seems to collapse in on her. Only a dim bulb set into the ceiling with a plastic cover gives them light. They're alone. Cassie shakes her head. Her sister is here somewhere. Cassie runs her hands along the door, testing for any sign of a hidden mechanism. She tries the knob. It rattles in her hand, locked.

"Cass..."

She shakes off Kierian's touch, wholly focused on her sister. "Viv?" Cassie calls. She puts everything she can into calling her sister's name, all the hope she can muster. She could be nearby. She might be able to hear her. "Viv? Viv!"

There is no reply. That's when her heart seizes. She hits the door hard then steps away. No one opens it. Nothing happens at all. Cassie takes a deep, shaking breath. Everything is upside down. Nothing is right and she can't do anything about it. Kierian stands close to her, but she keeps him at a distance.

"We have to find them," she says. There's a frenzy in her eyes. "We have to find her. I promised her that, you know I did. And if we're not there when they come back..."

"Cass," he says. He reaches out to her, but she backs a step away. Everything in her wants to fall apart – in burning sparks of rage, or a deep darkness, she's not quite sure. If it meant she could get her sister back, she would take either.

"I know what you promised her, and we aren't giving up," Kierian says. "She knows that too. We will find them, but for now we have to stay strong and wait. They'll be doing the same thing, I'm sure of it. Can you do that? For her?"

"I just want to know if she's okay." Cassie knows he's right, but to imagine her sister back in a dark place, so similar to the place she found her, breaks her heart. There's no way to find out. No closure to ease her heart. She just has to trust her sister is not alone.

"I know," Kierian says, his words soft. "If I could do anything I would. But as much as I can promise, we will find them."

"Thank you." She leans into him finally, his arms wrapping around her. She closes her eyes as he holds her, tears slipping down her cheeks. Everything hurts. Her arms and legs are sore, her stomach clenches, and she can't get her lungs to relax. Her heart seems to be stretched so far apart it threatens to break at any moment.

With nothing to measure time by but the light underneath the door, Cassie isn't sure how long it's been before a knock at the door causes both of them to jump. Kierian gently helps Cassie to her feet. Her heart leaps, but she stays close to him. She can't speak the hope that Vivian might be on the other side.

The door swings open and her fragile hope is shattered. One unseelie fae stands in the doorway, a soft purple to her veins and tint to her eyes. The bones lining her face and jaw jut out strongly, even more sunken even than the seelie. Cassie shivers as the fae's gaze settles on her.

"If you're expecting harm then I must apologize for the poor representation you've received of this court," the fae says. "I have come only to present a message."

"What do you want?" Kierian says.

"I'd like you to come with me," the fae says. Cassie has no doubt she's speaking to her. "It won't take long and I will return you here after. We simply have a proposition for you."

"We?" Cassie's question is covered by Kierian's voice.

"She's not going anywhere," he says. "Not alone." There's no room for argument in his tone.

The fae sighs. "Unlike the seelie, we prefer cordial discussion prior to rash action," the fae says. "As a princess in this court, I can assure you that my purpose for being here is approved and carries a sincere wish to have a civil conversation. But if you require us to use force, let that reflect your own choices and not a judgment of our hospitality."

Beyond the door, there are a number of guards standing behind the fae princess. As unwilling as she is, Cassie would rather walk than be dragged. She turns toward Kierian. His jaw is clenched, his focus shifting from her face to the fae she's turned her back on.

"I don't want to leave," Cassie says. Her words are quiet, only meant for him. "But this is not the time to fight. I have to go with them and trust they'll bring me back here."

"If you need me..."

"Then I'll reach out and tell you," Cassie says. "I trust you. I need you to trust me now too."

Kierian nods once, his lips slightly parted as if he has more to say but he doesn't. Cassie takes a deep breath, facing the princess still standing in the doorway.

"I'll come alone," Cassie says. "So long as you keep your word."

"I will," the princess says. "Please, right this way."

Cassie crosses the room, fighting the urge to look back at Kierian. She can feel the tension in their bond grow with every step. But the fae's eyes are on her, deep and focused in a way that could swallow her if she let it.

The door shuts behind her and Cassie lets out a breath. The princess leads her, flanked by guards, down the hall to another room. She shuffled quickly inside it. The unseelie princess stands opposite of her near a window. They're the only two in the room as the door shuts. She stands with her back to Cassie. It gives Cassie the moment to take in the dark violet dress she's wearing, the train of it spread out behind her and glittering in the soft light. It's as if she's cloaked in moonlight.

Finally, Cassie speaks. "You said you had a proposition for me." It's not a question, so she doesn't phrase it as one.

"You're sisters, aren't you? You and the other human girl we found."

The question drives a spike of fear through her heart, but Cassie answers honestly. "Yes."

"I know what it's like to have sisters. I know what it's like to have a sister who is in danger."

Cassie's heartbeat quickens. "What do you want from me?" The separation from her sister aches like a fissure through her heart. Talking to this fae about her doesn't feel good either, though she's not sure why.

The fae princess turns toward her. Her head is tilted slightly, as if she's studying Cassie. "You know what his clan is supposed to do when they imprint on a human, don't you?"

Cassie nods once.

"Then you know what danger your sister is in."

Cassie frowns slightly. "Her imprint tried to find her," she says, but the fae shakes her head.

"What did she say it felt like, last time she felt the bond?"

"What do you want from me?" Cassie asks again. "Not from my sister, what do you want from me?" She focuses on her breathing. It's the one thing she's sure of she controls in this moment.

"Simple," the princess says, a ghostly smile touching the edges of her lips. Even her pale lips and teeth seem to have a lavender sheen to them. "I offer you only one thing: a way to heal your sister and stop her from turning. To break the bond from the one she imprinted on. It will set her free from misery and protect her from further harm. They'll have no more claim to her, not her imprint and not their court. She'll be well and free."

The floor tilts underneath Cassie. Questions run through her head. It's picturing Vivian in her mind that outweighs everything else.

"She's going to turn?" Cassie can hardly speak the words.

"She will," the fae says.

"And you can stop it?"

"We can."

There's a pain in her chest, heat spreading over her body. If it's true, then she's failed her sister. She wasn't able to save her. Guilt floods through her, sealed by a vision of her sister with fangs.

The princess continues, a soft light coming through the window making her appear to glow. "All I ask is that you willingly join with me. With this court."

Cassie frowns. She forces her thoughts away from Vivian, and back to the fae's words. "Why do you want me to join you?"

The princess smiles, but it doesn't reach her eyes. "You humans always assume the story is about you as individuals, don't you?" she says. "I'm not offering you answers to your questions. I'm giving you a way to save your sister from the sentence she's been given unjustly."

Cassie shakes her head. Her strength doesn't return, but an inch of clarity does. "What's the price?" Cassie says. "What do you want in return for saving my sister?"

Chapter 17

KIERIAN IS ON HIS feet as soon as he hears footsteps approaching. He keeps his distance from the door, just enough that it can swing open without hitting him. He's waiting for Cassie. When the door opens, Kierian quickly scans the figures standing outside, but she isn't one of them.

"Where is she?" Kierian says. He sets his stare on the main fae who approaches him. She's different than the one who took Cassie, but that's only a passing fact in his mind.

"She will be back," the fae says. "But we need a moment with you first."

Kierian shakes his head. "I don't want anything from you."

The fae smiles. "Except for her." She'd look sickly if it wasn't for the way she carried herself – a posture perfected and a hunger in her purple eyes.

"She's not yours, and she's not yours to give."

The fae takes a step back, once again revealing a large number of guards behind her. "Will you come with me peacefully, or must I use force?"

He clenches his fists then flexes them. It's enough of a release that he steps forward without anger surging through him. "I'll come,"

Kierian says, his voice still low. "But she better be back when I return. Otherwise, you will need to use force."

"You don't need to deal in threats," the fae says, stepping aside so he can follow her into the hallway. "Though if that's the language you'd like to use I can certainly oblige. I have the authority, as a princess in this court. What would you prefer?"

"We can talk," Kierian says, forcing his tone even. "I think it would be better for both of us."

The new princess claps her hands. "Wonderful. Follow me."

She leads him down the hallway, the guards closing in tightly around him. Kierian can still feel their imprint. Cassie is alive. What he can't explain is the fact that as he's being led down the hall, the distance between himself and Cassie seems to shrink.

They pause halfway down a hallway, two doors at the end of it. The princess turns to face him. She's the same height as Kierian so she can't look down on him, but her stare holds the weight of someone who could.

"I need you to make me a promise," she says. Her voice is sweet as ever, but he doesn't trust a single word, much less all of them strung together.

"No."

She sighs. "Kier," she says, his name sending a chill through him. "Please. In order for me to be able to complete the task I was given, I need your cooperation."

"No."

"Do you want to see her? I can arrange that right now, but I need you to indulge me."

Those words nearly cause him to falter. He doesn't answer, his lips pressed together in a thin line. Still, his silence is an answer too.

"All I ask is you promise me silence and stillness while you see her," the princess says. "You will be reunited after."

His eyes betray him as he glances past her at the two doors at the end of the hall. He brings his focus back to the princess, but it's already been done. He does have one weakness and she knows what it is.

"Do you promise?"

He waits as long as he can, but the words still find their way out. "I promise," Kierian says. His stomach twists as she smiles.

"Good," she says, her face brightening. Kierian catches a glimpse of another door to his right as he follows the fae through the one in front of them. A voice spills out from the room.

"I'm not offering you answers to your questions. I'm giving you a way to save your sister from the sentence she's been given unjustly."

Kierian hardly hears the words. Cassie is here. She's just a few strides away from him. Immediately Kierian steps toward her, the tension between them drawing him in. The princess' hand closes around his shoulder. Kierian stops in his tracks despite the desire to close the distance, no matter the consequences. He made a promise. This is the price he pays – to be able to see her, hear her, but until this play is over, she can't see him.

Cassie stands tall, never breaking the unseelie's stare. Although she's across the room, she doesn't look at him. It's as if she can't see him, like he's invisible. His heart aches to call out to her. Still, he has the presence of mind to look back toward the door he came in and the other one that was beside it. That's when things become clearer. This place must have been built by unseelie hands. Kierian can tell from the etchings on the brick that there must be a false wall dividing this room in half, between the doors. He can see through this wall, but to Cassie it looks real.

Cassie shakes her head. "What's the price?" she says. "What do you want in return for saving my sister?"

The beauty of the other fae princess shifts then. Her smile turns to a bearing of teeth, flashing a mouth full of sharp edges. It's a shift that causes Kierian to bristle at his enemy's hands. He can see her form more truly than Cassie can, but this is a revealing of character as well as form.

"We are running out of time here, Cass," the fae says, something about her distinctly less feminine. "You must make a choice or else it will be made for you. If you're not willing to pay a price now, it won't matter what we name it. It is up to you to decide the kind of fate each of you will have going out from this place."

It's a show of intimidation. Kierian leans forward, careful to keep his feet rooted in place. He focuses on Cassie, pouring all his strength into her. She wavers but she does not break.

"I will not join you," Cassie says. Her voice shakes. "I cannot lose her, but I will not join you. I want her to have a sister to return to."

Kierian bows his head slightly. The tension in his body loosens and he closes his eyes. He can't speak the words, but there's a silent "thank you" on his lips. He doesn't know the recipient, but the words carry a weight he can't describe.

The princess in the other room composes herself, but the sharp edges of her personality don't disappear even as her features soften. "Then you will still pay a price," the fae says. "What you will reap from it will be far less pleasant than the offer you were made here. Don't forget that."

The fae's words, though vague, douses Kierian's relief. Still, he can't help but be proud. Cassie is still standing, unbroken. Weary, tired, he has no doubt. Despite it all, she's made her choice. She doesn't know, but he's so close. So close it's almost a physical pain to watch her leave. But as soon as she's gone, he can speak again.

He turns to fae princess standing behind him. "If you thought you would break me then you were wrong," Kierian says. There's a sharpness to his words.

"I thought it best to illustrate we're here to offer you something rather than simply be met with resistance," the fae says.

Kierian shakes his head. "I will not join you," he says, mirroring Cassie's reply. "She said it, and I say it now of my own will."

"Even if we could change the thing that keeps pulling you apart?"

Kierian chooses not to hear those words. They could mean anything, and there's something else he wants to know. "Why does her sister need saving?" he says.

"You're being hunted," she says, ignoring his question. "By your kind. While you're here you have a temporary shield, but as soon as you leave, you're at their mercy again. I have a feeling you know what that their brand of mercy looks like."

"If I lose my soul either way, does it really matter which hands take me?" Kierian says, his voice low. "She didn't answer her, so I'll ask you. What does it cost? If you want us to join you, if you want me to join you in exchange for this reward, what does it cost?"

The princess leans in. Kierian holds still as he can, her face resting above his left shoulder as she whispers in his ear. "What will it cost the rest of them if you decline? Is your soul worth more than that, or can you shoulder the burden of whatever the consequences may be? Lives are in your hands. Your imprint's, her sister's. What would you do to save them?"

There's a deep-set anger coursing through him. He'd like to imagine it's all directed at this princess, her court, but most of it is aimed at himself. "What have you done to her sister?" Kierian says. "Why does Vivian need saving?"

As soon as the words leave his mouth, everything seems to stand still. The scene becomes a picture. If only it could be a moment in time he could bury and retake. But his confidence cracks as the impact of his words takes hold.

Kierian can't move. The fae steps back a few paces, a smile growing on her face. "Vivian," she says, holding the name on her tongue for a moment. "Is not your current concern. Though, I suppose if you were pardoned the danger to her life would cease too, wouldn't it? You could save her from her fate."

Kierian absorbs the words being spoken to him through the torrent of thoughts inside his head. Any of the rage still left within him, all the revitalization from seeing Cassie, drains from him.

"And what would you do?" Kierian says finally. "Offer me your cup of mercy? I don't believe your definition of mercy is one I want to partake of either."

The princess smiles, a softness that's not helped by the razor sharpness of her teeth. "You don't know that. Why would we bring you here, make this offer, if we didn't intend to keep it?"

Kierian closes his eyes. Cassie. Where is she? How...

"I need you to look at me."

Kierian jumps, the fae standing right beside him. Her voice breaks his concentration. Her sharp fierceness is leveled at him, and he struggles to bear the weight of her stare.

"They're being hunted because of what you are," she says. "No matter how far you run there will always be someone chasing you. You should know that. You can't outrun what you are, not by your own power. We can suppress the disease that's in you, creating your vampiric traits. It will suppress your bond, but if they can no longer claim you as their own it will set you free. Your freedom wins theirs too."

The memory of breathing echoes through his chest. He would have wanted that once. In the first few weeks, months even, there was nothing he wanted more than to become human again. He was too scared to fight for the life that was his. He ran from it. The vampire court took advantage of him in a state of panic and vulnerability, and he believed their lies instead of fighting for his life. That clan claimed him as their own and he let them.

"Free?" Kierian says. His voice cracks. "I haven't been free since the day I saw what this world looks like, since I was beaten, scared, and believed I had nowhere else to go except to take what was given to me when they forcibly made me what I am. You say that you can do something that will release me from the bondage of my clan, stripping me of the burden of becoming a mythic? You can't do that. If I accepted, I'd be bound to you. I'd rather face an evil I know intimately well than to subject myself to one unknown."

His words are a shield of glass. To even think about Cassie means the crack in his heart widens. Reliving the past opens old wounds, ones still festering and diseased that were never allowed to heal. Moments he vowed he would never take root in him have shaped who he has become, even if he turns a blind eye to them. But what matters is he came here alongside Cassie, Vivian, Flora, and Bayler. That's how he intends to walk out, no matter the wages it costs to see that happen.

The princess' silence weighs heavy on him. Kierian forces the rest of his story to stay inside himself and not spill it at the feet of someone who would certainly use those words against him. The fae holds him in anticipation, her lips slightly parted as she breathes.

"Thank you," the princess says finally. Before Kierian can react, she continues. "Guards! Take him back. We're finished here."

The door to the room opens, but Kierian's eyes are still on the princess. "That's it then?" he says. "We're done here?"

Hands close on his shoulders, pulling him away. The princess smiles sweetly at him. "I'll receive you if you'd like to meet with me again," she says. "Until then, I don't believe anything else I have to say can change your mind. Let me know if you'd like to prove me wrong."

Her eyes don't leave him until the door shuts. Kierian doesn't say another word, and yet her voice seems to echo in his head, following him as the guards lead him down the hall. He won't change his mind, but he would like to prove her wrong. The unseelie can't save him, no matter what they promise. But can he save the rest of his friends? Kierian has no answer, only a darkness that rises within him in response. He could drown in it if he let himself.

***

Cassie is pushed unceremoniously into the dim room. She trips, hitting the ground hard. By the time she scans the space, the door is already closing and she realizes she's all alone. She runs back to the door, pulling on the handle moments after it's locked. Panic spikes through her body, her heart beating rapidly. "Where is he?" she shouts. "Where is he!" No one answers.

She's exhausted when she finally lets herself collapse on the floor. She aches. But as she sits, she realizes it's not only her body. It's her heart too. It's her bond. She frowns, reaching out for it. There's a draw toward Kierian like there always is, but something is different. A thud echoes from the hallway and she jumps to her feet. Cassie stands there at the door, watching, waiting, but it doesn't open. She can't hear anything, but it's as if she can feel him on the other side.

"Kier? Are you there?"

There's no answer, not from him or anyone else. She puts a hand on the door, though the wood can't give her any answers. In the absence of any other sound, she tests the door handle. It twists in her hand. Cassie lets go of it quickly, her pulse picking up. Did they do that on purpose? And the question she wants to ask even less – what will she find on the other side?

Cassie opens the door gently. It swings inward, revealing an empty, dim hallway. There, sitting with his head down and cross-legged on the floor, is Kierian.

"Kier?" She crouches in the doorway, reaching a hand toward him. He stiffens at her touch. She frowns, pulling back slightly.

"Are you okay?" she asks. The answer is clear, but without a reply from him she can't do or say anything more helpful. She looks around but there's no one watching them. As far as she can tell, they really are alone.

"I'm here," Cassie says. "I'm not going anywhere."

Finally, excruciatingly slow, Kierian looks up at her. His face is wet, eyes hardly able to meet hers. "I saw you," he says, his voice a whisper. "Just before they tried to scare you into accepting. It was a false wall, just like the bar. I couldn't talk to you, but I heard them say something about your sister. And when you left..." His voice trails off and his head falls again.

"Kier..."

"I messed up. They know her name. I'm so sorry. I didn't know how to face you again if I can't take that back. And if we run..."

Their bond feels so fragile, like a thin cord instead of rope. If she were to touch it she's afraid it might fray or snap. But despite everything, she holds onto it. She lays her hand on his arm.

"Then what are we going to do about it?" Cassie says.

Kierian looks up at her, frowning. "What?"

She takes a deep breath. "What are we going to do about it? You told them her name. We're not joining them. Like you started to say, I don't think running is going to solve this. So, what are we going to do now?"

He hesitates. "You're not angry?"

Cassie takes another deep breath. "I think I am," she says, then shakes her head. "I know am. But I'm not willing to let that divide us. That just means they win, right?"

It's then that Kierian lifts his hands from the floor but stops mid-motion. "May I?" he asks.

She softens at his question. "I was waiting for you to ask." Cassie pulls him into a hug, holding him as they sit in the doorway. He holds tightly to her, arms wrapped tightly around each other.

She can't reach her sister. She wants to, desperately. She's angry at him. There's no purpose in denying it. She trusted him with that knowledge and now it's in their hands. But there are things the fae can offer, things they can take, and some things they can never control. This is one of those things she will not let them have.

Chapter 18

Footsteps echo down the hall. Vivian can hear the other two seelie shifting in the cell. She keeps her eyes closed, her body still shaking. No matter how hard she fights it, she can't stop. Even as a new voice speaks, Vivian remains curled on the floor, her arms wrapped tightly around herself.

"You'll have your time, each of you," says a feminine voice. "But first we'd like to talk to the girl."

"We don't want anything from you," Flora says. "And you're not separating us."

Vivian focuses on breathing in and out, the feeling of her chest rising and falling. The concrete is cold beneath her.

"You might not think you want anything," says the woman. "But we offer the kindness to still present that choice. She can either come willingly or by force. That decision is hers and hers alone."

Vivian squeezes her eyes shut tighter, the black of her vision starting to form little pixels against the back of her eyelids. If only all of this would disappear.

"She's here," Bayler says. "Why does she have to be alone?"

"We have our reasons. But I need to hear from her. What is her answer?"

Finally, Vivian opens her eyes. There's so much weight on her shoulders, on her chest. Her legs feel like lead. But she does need to answer.

"I wanted to come," Vivian says softly, her voice wavering. "I think this is where I have to show I meant it."

"Viv..." Flora cuts herself off quickly.

Vivian pulls herself up, her hands clasped in front of her. "I'm okay," she says. Her eyes are still on the ground at her feet.

"You don't have to do this," Bayler says. Despite everything, Vivian smiles.

"No," she says. Her hands shake along the same frequency as her voice. "I don't have to, but I can. I will."

Vivian can't make any of this go back to normal. Nothing can go back to the way it was. She can't change any of it, but at this moment she's not alone. At least for a little while, she will be out of this cold, dark cell.

"Follow me," the unseelie woman says.

Vivian steps out of the cell. The pressure on her lungs lightens and she takes a deep breath. She flinches as the cell is locked behind her.

"Come."

There's nowhere else for Vivian to go. She follows the unseelie woman up a flight of stairs into a room with small oval windows lining the top of the far wall. The rest of the stone is a mural, wrapping around the entire space. Vivian can't help but be drawn to the picture that expands from behind the fae, filling the room.

The mural is one continuous scene. The style feels ancient, but the colors are vivid. What Vivian can only imagine is a warrior queen rises behind the fae, her body filling the height of the wall. The painted sickle in her hand touches the ceiling. A flowing gown spills around her feet, the train of it thicker and more decorative than the one the real fae in front of her is wearing. A battle unfolds along the other walls of the room, overlaid on a jungle background. But what Vivian can't look away from is the face of the warrior queen.

It's different from the fae she's seen so far. The painted woman's skin is like an insect's armor - a praying mantis. Two long antennae are curled and in two spirals atop her head, a beetle-like jaw and mouth, and huge black eyes. The tint of the woman's skin is the same color of the eyes as the fae standing in front of her – she looks almost human. Against this fantastical background, Vivian can't help but wonder if this is what this fae really looks like. Something deep inside her says this portrait is what she's supposed to be seeing. Which, considering everything, she's both ready and not ready to believe.

"It's a stunning depiction, isn't it?" The fae's voice startles Vivian, drawing her attention.

"Is that what you really look like?" Vivian says. She can't help but ask, even if she dreads the answer.

The fae smiles. "It is, though even a mythic's first imprint can't see us in all our true beauty. By your question, though, I would venture to guess you're not the first or even second human your mythic has imprinted on."

Something recoils in Vivian at the use of the word 'your.' "No." Her voice carries strongly, but her muscles start to tense. That vampire is no more hers than she is his.

The fae nods. "I understand. Not every human who imprints on a mythic is lucky enough to find one like your sister's vampire friend."

Vivian's hands ball into fists. Trapped. That word screams in her head, fills her veins with a panic that only continues to rise. But the only way out means she can't fall apart now. She has to hold on, just like her sister said.

"You said I had a choice," Vivian says, pushing the words out. "What is that choice?"

"I was hoping to reveal more of this world to you, if you would have liked," the fae says. "This is the best place to do it. But, to put it succinctly, you have an imprint. A bond. The past cannot be changed but having arrived here, we can change what happens going forward. We're offering you the ability to break that bond. You will no longer be able to see this world but you will not be imprinted on the one who gave you this sight. Their power over you will cease. We can make all of it go away. All we want in return is for you to stand with our court. Let us help you. We can't right every wrong, but we can provide a balm."

Vivian doesn't reach for the bond. It's there, but she's built a wall to keep it back. Instead, there's a warmth in the pit of her stomach. The warmth is fueled by anger, by pain. She doesn't really want to extinguish it. She's already been through more than she thought possible, more than she thought was real. It's too much for her to comprehend at once.

Vivian would like to do something that would make them hurt. She wants them to know what they've put her through. The vampires, these fae, all of them. In some sense, that's what this fae is offering her: control. She's already been hurt, she's already seen all this, and she's a part of it. If she gives that up to this court then she's not free of anything at all. Someone else will still have power over her. She can only get hurt again.

Vivian opens her eyes, breathing deeply as she meets the fae's gaze. "I don't know why you would want me to join you," she says, voice wavering. "But no matter what you offer me, it won't be enough."

The fae smiles softly and Vivian's heart lurches. Despite the anger, the calloused wounds inside her, there's something even more enticing about that softness. She longs for it.

"Are you sure?" the fae asks sweetly. "There's so much we could do for you. Do you know what that would mean? Do you know what we could do to them?"

For a moment, Vivian lets herself fall into the illusion. She's tired and hurt. There could be safety here. But what would that really mean? There's Cassie, but also Flora and Bayler. Kierian, though his name still makes her shutter. She could be safe, but the cost... There's still no gain that could make it worth it, no matter how fiery or full of ashes her heart is. Nothing can fix what's already been broken. They can't put her back together again.

"I don't need to know," Vivian says finally. "My answer is no."

Vivian braces herself, one hand reaching out to steady herself against the wall. For a moment, a sense of dread takes hold of her, something dark filling the room. Then it recedes just as quickly as it came.

"I'll accept your choice, now that you know what's at stake," the fae says. "But you're free to change your mind. All you need to do is tell me. Don't forget that, no matter what comes next." Though they're spoken softly, the words do nothing to calm Vivian.

The fae crosses the room, her eyes on Vivian until she's passed. Vivian glances once more at the painting on the far side, then follows the fae out the door. Vivian retreats into her thoughts as she's led down the hall. Even as she's made her choice, the fae's words echo in her mind. What could they do? It's an open-ended threat and a comfort.

***

Flora is standing in the center of the cell when the guards bring Vivian back. Bayler is gone. Vivian's shaking returns slightly, but she doesn't speak when she meets Flora's eyes.

Flora steps forward as the door is opened. The unseelie fae raises a hand. "Stay back," she says. "You'll have your time, but not yet."

As soon as she's able, Vivian bolts into Flora. Flora stumbles back a few steps, but the two of them stay upright. Vivian holds on tight, even as the door locks and footsteps retreat behind her. It's Flora who gently pulls back first.

"Are you okay?" Flora asks. "What happened?"

Vivian takes a deep breath. "I'm okay," she says. A shiver runs down her spine, but she can speak once it passes. "I know what they are."

Vivian can't read the expression on Flora's face that follows. "Then you know what I am too," Flora says finally. "Almost, but I'm not so different."

The words aren't ones Vivian wants to dwell on. "And they asked me to join them. If I did, they would break the imprint."

Flora nods but doesn't speak. Vivian's hands are still shaking. "I told them no," Vivian says. "I couldn't say yes, no matter what they promised, right? Anything they said would have been a lie." She believes the words, but even as she speaks, she can feel herself leaning forward waiting for Flora's response.

"I think you made the right choice," Flora says. She's staring just above Vivian's shoulder. "I just wish it wasn't at that price. I wish we could make that happen any other way." A silence settles, but Vivian still waits.

"Flora?"

The fae takes a deep breath, still not meeting Vivian's eyes. "They could have done what I can't. Maybe they really could help you. Is it worth risking yourself to find out? To find out what price they would require of you? I would have made the same choice if I were you, but none of this makes any sense. Why do they want you?"

The question isn't really aimed at her. Vivian knows that, but it still hurts. Flora won't look at her. Despite the confines of the cell there seems to be a larger-than-life distance between them. She keeps waiting for Flora to say something else. Anything else. The words never come, and the distance seems to grow. Vivian crosses to the far side of the room, lowering herself to the ground with her back against the solid wall.

"Why do they want you?" Vivian asks. Her question is a whisper, one she's sure Flora hears. Flora never answers and Vivian doesn't ask again. Her wonder at the possibilities to that question causes her thoughts to spiral down darker paths the longer time goes on.

Chapter 19

VIVIAN WANTS THE DRESS the unseelie gave her to be itchy, too heavy. If at least one thing is wrong with it, she can focus all her emotions on that thing. But she can't find one fault. The sleeves end in triangle lace over the back of her hands, the soft lavender color covering her from just below her collar bone to the tips of her shoes. Despite the hands that pushed it through the bars, despite the hands she's sure made it, it's a beautiful dress. She'd just rather be anywhere but here in it.

Flora's dress is a deeper color of violet, reminiscent of a midnight glow. It starts at the base of Flora's neck, covering her arms and fitting closer than Vivian's as it falls to the floor, a slight train behind it. A deep frown has settled onto Flora's face and Vivian hasn't had the courage to ask her why yet.

"They're taunting us," Flora says. She's so quiet Vivian almost misses the words.

"What do you mean?" Vivian says. Her fingers twist the lace of her dress.

"The color," Flora says. "They don't do anything on accident. Purple is the color of royalty in their court, one they hold as sacred. It's good for them. For the seelie, it saps our strength. It hides who we are, dims us, so that we become just a little more like them."

Vivian hesitates, but ventures to ask another question when Flora doesn't continue. "Then why wear it at all?"

Flora shakes her head. "I don't know what game they're playing," she says. "We're meeting them on their terms, trying to follow their rules. If I thought it would do any good, I would have refused. I got us into this mess, though. I dragged each of you with me, willingly or not. I can't put the rest of you at risk for the sake of my pride."

"A sound choice." The voice comes from down the hall. The unseelie's violet eyes are somewhere between the shades Vivian and Flora wear. "I trust you'll keep that wisdom in mind through this proceeding. If you would come with me..."

A guard unlocks the cell. Bayler is still nowhere to be seen. Still, the door swinging open into an illusion of freedom sends a dark thrill through Vivian. No one touches her as she steps out of the cell. There's not a hand on her as they're led down the hall, though they're surrounded on every side.

The soldiers stop at a set of solid wooden doors. The tops of them arch toward the angled ceiling, seeming to have been cut out of a single piece of wood. It would have to be a tree taller than any Vivian has ever seen. There aren't any patterns or decorations to the door, just its hinges and handles set into them. Despite the nervous energy wrapping itself around her bones, Vivian is struck by the simple beauty of it. It draws her in, and that's what worries her.

"This is as far as I go," the violet-eyed fae says, stepping out of the way. "The rest is up to you."

"What is it you want from me?" Flora says.

"It's not what I want with you," the unseelie fae says. "I believe you've met our king and queen before. It's what they want from you that matters."

Before Vivian can make sense of the words, and before Flora replies, the doors in front of them are pushed open. The sounds, features, smells, and the overwhelming presence of a thick crowd causes Vivian's chest to tighten. Her breathing begins to quicken as Flora takes the first step into the room. The sea of unseelie fae parts, a narrow path forming. All of them are watching. Vivian can feel the weight of their eyes. Murmured conversations swirl around her but Vivian can't keep track of them. At the far end of the room, there's a raised platform, steps leading up to it like a stage. Two figures are there, half concealed in shadows. They each sit on a golden throne, violet inlaid into it. Fit for a king and queen. Every sound apart from Vivian's heartbeat quiets as a hand raises from one of the thrones.

"Thank you all for joining us here today," a feminine voice says, echoing across the room. The queen. "Each of you is an esteemed guest, honoring us with your presence. This is not a moment of frivolity, of pleasure with no purpose besides itself. No, this is much more than that.

"We have long acquainted ourselves with shadows. Contented ourselves with shadows. And though we know them, they have not been ours to wield. We have been bound by them. The time has come that our brethren cannot bind us, nor can rules set in place over us govern us. There is a veil, but we have the power to break it to those who we choose. We may not be able to rend it completely, but let any remaining doubt be dispelled as this evening unfolds. It is now our tool to wield. It is ours to reveal."

Every word washes over Vivian like a cold wind, drawing warmth out of her body. Voices rise as whispers, growing louder and echoing off the walls. The volume seems to spike to levels Vivian's ears can hardly handle. Flora's hand on her shoulder causes her to wince, but she does not shake off the touch. Instead, she falls in step with Flora as they continue to pass through the room.

Vivian and Flora stop once they reach the stairs at the foot of the stage. Flora lets go of her and Vivian dares to look up from the ground. The first thing she notices is their eyes. The other fae had a light lavender iris, a soft purple hue. Underneath elaborate crowns, jewels dripping from them, these fae stare at her with a striking deep violet gaze.

Vivian has seen the king once before now, but not like this. His gaze is cast out toward the crowd. It lets her see the harsh lines of his face, deep pockets of shadow in his cheeks, and bony hands gripping the armrest with force. It's all at odds with the small, warm smile he gives.

Vivian glances to the right and a chill runs through her as she meets the queen's eyes. Even as the queen's gaze drifts over her, there's something lingering. It's as if she doesn't need to keep looking at Vivian to see something - to see through her. It's almost more unsettling to try and determine where the pale, ivory lace stops and the queen's skin begins.

The queen holds up a hand again, drawing the attention of the whole room, including the king. Her voice carries but her gaze settles on Flora. "Here we have before us a representative of the seelie court," the queen says. Her voice quiets all remaining whispers. "What message have you come to bear?"

Flora lifts her chin slightly. "I am no longer a representative or member of the seelie court," Flora says. "I bear no message on behalf of another."

"Then for what purpose have you come?" the queen says. There's an even tone to her words. Vivian wonders if she already knows the answers to the questions she's asking.

"Not to stand before you here," Flora says. If Vivian couldn't see Flora's hands clasped tightly behind her back, knuckles white, she'd almost believe Flora was speaking with confidence. "I know of your court's plans. I was willing to do whatever it cost me to undermine your plans of mass revelation. I still am." Flora hesitates before speaking those last three words.

The king's smile grows wider. It's a slow movement, made only slightly less terrifying when his grin stops growing. "Good," he says. The word is long drawn out. Vivian has to remind herself to breathe as she waits for him to finish, the space between each word excruciatingly long. "Even in the face of certain failure you are still willing to try. That will serve you well here."

A slight shuffling draws Vivian's attention. Despite her better judgement, she looks over. It's Cassie. She's standing next to the vampire. There's too much distance between her and Cassie to close the distance, even if she wasn't terrified of moving. She can see Cassie's face, lips slightly parted, but Vivian can't catch her attention. Still, knowing her sister is here is some comfort.

"I think you misunderstand me," Flora says. "I serve no court, nor did I come here to join one."

"You have not yet heard our offer," the king says. "The prince over the seelie did not listen. His is a game of arrogance and pride. He holds steadfast to rules he believes will protect him. They will become his undoing. The rest of his court will follow after. But you? Standing in his shadow, chosen not risen to rank - what better message could we send beyond war than turning you against him? He deserves it, doesn't he?"

Flora stiffens. "If you knew he would not listen, why all the theatrics? Break the accords if you hold them to that much disdain, if you have no use for peace. The responsibility and consequence rests on your shoulders. If you want to define your own freedom, your own control, why not simply take it? What is the purpose in waiting?"

"Tell me," the king says. He leans back against the throne. "Who put the accords into writing, determining the stretch of our kingdom?"

"Both sides agreed to the terms set. Each royal of our courts signed it. Unless you don't remember."

"I remember signing it with seelie daggers poised at our throats," the king says. "I think you're too young to remember it quite like that, though. It was never about peace. It was about control. While your prince was there, I don't remember you. Though I'm sure his retelling of the event that occurred in his childhood was untainted truth."

"Fighting what's written in those accords won't change them or the circumstances they were signed under," Flora says. "It won't set you free."

"We do not want to be set free," the king says. "To be set free is to be seated underneath another power higher. Breaking the accords is the only way to reseat ourselves as a high power."

"For what?" Flora says. "For the glory of your own thrones? It can't last forever. Even we aren't immortal."

Silence stretches as the king's gaze bores into Flora. His voice is soft, just above a whisper. "What else can be lost?" he says. "Those who cannot see past the veil. You would be standing here alone if not for the parting of that veil. Everyone else? They remain blinded, held captive without the knowledge they are bound. Does that protect them? Keep them safe? What mercy is it to them to keep it hidden?"

The king's voice rises, ending in a shout. "No, we will not be set free, but we will set humankind free. Fae hands may not have been the one to put that veil in place, but by unseelie hands we will tear it down!"

Vivian's hands begin to shake. She clasps them together, holding them close to her stomach. There's a tremor inside her too, one that's beyond her control. It wraps itself around her. She can feel a thread around her wrists, around her neck. He's looking for her again. He revealed this world to her, showed her the violence of it. Even with her eyes closed she can't unsee what's been done. If it had stayed hidden from her that would have been a larger mercy than she or these fae could ever know.

Flora's voice shakes, but she addresses the crowd as she meets the queen's gaze. "What do you call mercy? What is your vision of peace, or of power? Whatever it is you want from me, if your motives are pure, I will submit myself to whatever it is you request of me. But if peace and mercy to your eyes are beyond recognizable to me, I will refuse. I know the difference between what is good and evil. I may struggle with the good, but I will not fall to evil."

"Oh, Flora," the queen says. "Haven't you learned anything? All this time and you still don't know you were chosen." Her voice is slow and sweet, a beckoning that's hard to ignore.

"What is it that you want from me?" Flora says. Her words are metered, trying to hide the wavering of her voice, but Vivian can hear the truth. "You said before it's your time to take back what you feel is owed you. What, then, could I possibly give that you haven't already set your eyes upon to take for yourselves?"

"I am not your enemy, Flora," the queen says. "We are not your enemy. We want you here. What more do you need than that freely offered invitation? You've won and lost so much to get here. It's the least we can give you."

Flora shakes her head. "I do not stand with you," she says. Her voice is low, unfiltered emotion behind her words. "I will not stand with you, and I will not stand with the seelie court. And still, I do not stand alone."

The warmth that floods Vivian from Flora's statement doesn't last long, shattered in the wake of the royals' next words.

"We offered your friends a choice," the queen says. "We offered them their desires, in whatever form they might take, in exchange for their loyalty. You are right. This is larger than what any one of them or what they could offer. But you, Flora, don't underestimate the role you might play in this story. If you cannot believe us now, let us show you the difference between a vision of rejection and a vision of hope. If we can't win you, you've given us all we need to break you."

Chapter 20

KIERAN CAN HARDLY HOLD all the tension coursing through his body. He's acutely aware of where Cassie is standing, the seconds it would take to shield her if needed. There's a solid row of fae behind them. Their best escape route would be up onto and across the stage. The only other option he can think of is to fight their way through the sea of unseelie, and he can't imagine that would go well.

Kierian has seen Flora break before. Never in the moment, only after. That's what he holds on to. Despite how she holds her composure, he can't help but look for signs she's giving out. Flora has held her ground. She's refused their call. And yet they won't relent. Press hard enough, in the right way, and anyone has the potential to cave.

The queen looks to her left, the first time she's looked anywhere but the crowd or at Flora. Whispers go up from the crowd, but Kierian doesn't try and decipher them. Instead, his gaze locks onto the figure that steps out of the shadows, head bent, stopping behind the two thrones. One of Kierian's hands balls into a fist. He squeezes Cassie's hand once with the other.

Bayler.

"Traitor." Kierian mutters the word under his breath, despite his desire to let the fae hear him. It's Bayler's refusal to meet their eyes that makes Kierian wish even more the seelie could hear him. But where they're standing is incredibly fragile ground. It's only Cassie's pulse, carried as an echo along their bond, that keeps him grounded.

"One friend," the queen says, gesturing lightly toward Bayler. "Chose the better way. The others refused, despite the nature of our offer. Consider the reasons why. If they have paid a steep price to stand beside you, what does their sacrifice earn them?"

Flora's voice is low as she speaks, taking one step toward Bayler. "What is it they offered that you could not turn down? Can you live with the choice you've made?"

Eyes on the ground, Bayler's lips part. Kierian leans forward to hear, but the queen rests a hand on Bayler before he can speak.

"What reward could you possibly offer in light of what the rest of them have given up for you?" the queen says. Though her voice is sweet, she wields her words like a knife. Even Kierian can feel the weight of the queen's statement. He can see Flora flinch. She doesn't know. She doesn't know what it costs them to stand by her, but they're here in despite it all.

"If you have something specific to offer me beyond vague threats, guilt, and shame, say it in plain words. Make it clear," Flora says, emotion building in her voice as she speaks. "Allow me to waste less of your time and less of my breath to reject your proposal and move on to what comes next. There is nothing you can offer me that will tempt me enough to betray myself."

Flora's hands are clenched, head titled upward in her anger as she addresses the queen. Kierian is certain there's a rage coursing through her he can only imagine. It's the resentment in every word, in her voice, that worries him.

"What were you?" the king says. Flora's oppressive glare snaps toward him when he speaks. "A servant in your own court, bound to someone else's will? A messenger between courts, an appointed position but one in which you still had no power? You were still a pawn to the prince. We offer you a place in this court. Position. Power. Everything that your court could never, would never, offer you.

"You were nothing. They never saw you. They never listened to you. If they did, would you be here now? Would you have been driven to the measures that have brought you here? I don't believe so. Dear Flora, where are you now? You have inadequate leverage to state your demands, followed by few who I can only imagine have given up much but have gained little to be by your side, and still powerless to achieve what you came here to do. But that doesn't have to be true any longer. There will be war, things put in motion will ensure that, but we will not cast you out. We are the ones who sought you. We want you at our side to help lead."

Flora puts a foot on the bottom step. No one stops her, her voice the only sound in the whole room. "You offer me a place here. You offer me power," Flora says. Her voice comes out a snarl, as if the words are a disgrace to speak. "You attempt to define what you do now know. Who you do not know. You serve veiled threats, seeking to turn my allies against me to earn my allegiance. For someone who believes they have something to be free from, what you offer me is bondage.

"Tear me down. I've already wandered those paths in my mind for far too many years. There's no hope within your walls. Not for me, and not for my friends. You continue to remind me I should know better. I do. If I cannot save those who do not know what they need saving from..."

"Would you sacrifice those who know exactly what it has cost them to ally themselves with you?" The queen's voice, ice cold and without hesitation, cuts through Flora's rambling.

Hands clasp Kierian's shoulder. His attention was so drawn to Flora that he lost focus. He can only catch a brief glimpse of Cassie before he's wretched from her, fae bodies separating them. Kierian twists toward the ones restraining him, a low growl from his throat. He's met with a swift kick, bringing him to the ground and landing hard on his knees. He can now only see Flora, taking one more step up the stairs as the royals look down on her.

"Is that what I'm worth?" Flora says. "Three lives and one that's managed to save himself?"

Her words are hollow. Kierian shakes his head slightly though she can't see him. She's faltering. Her voice shakes. Her hands rest at her waist, but she has no weapon to reach for. If he can't believe the words she's saying, he's certain the king and queen can see right through her.

A scream cuts through the stiff silence, cutting it like a knife. "Viv!" Cassie's voice, cut short as she cries out. A thud lands a short distance from Kierian. He bucks against the hands restraining him. He can still feel their imprint. Cassie is alive. That's all he knows for certain.

Flora whips around sharply. It's seeing her face that nearly causes Kierian to crack. Fear. Her eyes dart quickly between each of them. Kierian doesn't dare speak. His silence is the only way he knows to prevent any of them from coming to more harm.

"It's effective, isn't it?" the queen says. "Maybe you are worth more, but four lives are all we have. They're not the only ones, though, are they? Your imprint is dead already. Can you live with the blood of these three on your hands as well? With the blood of any who would follow you on this hopeless pursuit of resistance?"

"I didn't kill him!" Flora shouts. She turns sharply back toward the queen. She breathes deeply, her voice slightly calmer when she continues. "My imprint didn't die at my hands." She backs down one step, but the fae in the audience flood forward, blocking her retreat. The only place she can go is up.

"But you know who took his life," the queen says. The sweetness in her voice verges on sinister. There's a dangerous glimmer in her eye now, leaning forward as if to devour Flora whole. "This is your last offer. Stand with us. Offer us the best of what you can do. Tell us what you know. You'll get to make that prince pay for what he's done. Give him everything he deserves. But we're not so cruel to our own, not if you come willingly. Choose one of these three to be your confidant, despite their denial. The other two will live, you'll be free to ensure that."

A beat of silence passes, the whole room seeming to hold its breath. Flora's chest rises and falls quickly.

"And if I refuse?" Flora whispers the question.

The queen shrugs. "We tell the seelie court what they want to hear. You knew exactly what you were doing. You walked away from your court to join ours. An exchange of secrets for a place of power, equal to if not greater than that prince's. We granted it. Then we had everything we needed to create the war you warned him of. He should have listened before, but I'm sure he'll listen now. And, of course, we will take care of these three. See, the methods of it don't matter so much if the outcome is the same. The amount of blood shed as a precursor to the inevitable is in your hands, Flora."

Flora looks back one more time. Kierian opens his mouth to speak, but the words don't come before she's looked away. She bows her head, turning back to the unseelie fae on their thrones.

"Flora," the king says. He draws her name out, speaking so slowly it's antagonizing to wait for him to finish. "What is your choice?"

"I..."

"Please." Out of the quiet is one word Vivian whispers over and over again. Kierian can't tell if she knows she's saying the word out loud, but her plea is not restrained.

Flora curls further inward on herself. "Whatever blood may be on my hands, I will not let theirs be added to it," Flora says. "If the cost of saving their lives is to stand by your side, then I accept. For their sake, not any others."

If they could just start over. If they knew what would lie ahead from the beginning maybe they wouldn't have ended up in this trap. Maybe it was doomed from the beginning. But if she breaks, if she's broken... Kierian's not quite sure what he's doing here anymore. He can still feel Cassie's heart beating. It's the only thing that reminds him he's still alive, if only barely.

As the thought runs through his mind, the hands holding him let go. Before he can stand, Cassie is by his side, kneeling with him. She's not looking at him, though. He turns to find Vivian, still alive and standing. That's one small relief.

The queen's words bring him back to the present. "As you wish. Who then do you choose as your confidant, as you take your place in this court?"

Flora turns around slowly. She looks at each of them, her eyes glazed over. She is not herself. There are no tears shed, but she has made her choice. Kierian may still be alive, but he's not sure why.

"Viv," Flora says.

Cassie gasps, struggling to stand and move toward her sister. Kierian holds her back, his arms wrapping around her waist as she tries to push away from him.

"Viv," Cassie says. "Viv, please."

Their bond pulses rapidly, shaking. All he can do is hold her as her breaths hitch. He leans into her. If this is the last moment he can protect her, he will do so with all the strength he has left in him.

Vivian doesn't say a word, she only nods at Flora. The tension in the room is thick, but there's no reservation to Vivian's movements as she climbs the steps to Flora's side. She doesn't look back. Kierian's not sure if he wishes she would, if only for Cassie's sake, or if that would make it harder. Flora and Vivian together face the royals. Cassie leans back hard against him, her lips moving but no sound coming from her.

The queen claps her hands together. Kierian jumps at the sudden sound. "Good," she says. "It's been decided. Bayler, take Vivian to the back rooms with the rest of the assistants and help her get situated. Flora, you'll take your place and remain here beside us. A spot will be made for you shortly."

Cassie flinches at her sister's name. Kierian holds her tighter. She doesn't fight him. They don't have anywhere else to go.

"Now," the king says. "We celebrate!"

A roar erupts from the crowd, music flooding the room and overwhelming every other sense. Kierian can feel every note from the strings. He keeps his eyes alert, scanning for any threats that would reach them.

"My sister." Cassie's voice hardly reaches him.

"I'm sorry," Kierian says. There aren't enough words or time for him to tell her how fully he means those words. "I'm so, so sorry. She's not alone, though. Flora will help take care of her, just like we will take care of each other, okay? They can separate us, but they can't divide us."

She shakes her head. "But what if they do?" Cassie says. "They already did. What's stopping them from doing it again?"

There's a darkness overshadowing their bond, swirling in the invisible space between them. Kierian gently tilts her face to look at him. All the words he wishes he could say melt away, but he grasps at what he can. He has to believe it's enough.

"You went to the ends of the earth for your sister," Kierian says. "You had no business trusting me, but you did anyway. We chose to follow Flora, same as Bayler. But you cannot forget that it's you, Viv, and Flora I am fighting for. I need you to trust me. They can't divide us if we refuse to let doubt in."

Hands pull Kierian upright. The force pulls Cassie up with him. There's only enough time for Kierian to see Cassie's wide eyes as they pull her from him again before a fist impacts his stomach. He doubles over in pain.

"Kier!" He hears his name. "Kier!" Cassie's voice is further this time.

Kierian rights himself, seeking out Cassie even as he's pushed toward the other side of the room. He catches one last glimpse of her across the room before she disappears through a set of doors. All that's left is the sea of unseelie and Flora, head bowed as she stands at the left side of the thrones.

"You have to believe this isn't the end. This is not the end," Kierian says. He's not sure who the words are meant for, or why he says them, but he holds onto the little hope they suggest with everything he has left.

ALTERED

The Imprinted Trilogy, Book 2

Brooke Stemme

Altered

Chapter 1

Vivian's heart races in her chest. All around her voices rise, mixing into an indecipherable buzz. It's as if a force outside herself caused her to climb these steps up to the feet of the unseelie thrones. Two violet eyed fae stare back at her, their smiles not reaching their eyes. Vivian isn't looking at them.

Between and behind their thrones is Flora. Her hazel eyes meet Vivian's, an acknowledgeable of this moment. Flora, against her will standing by their side in order to save the rest of their lives. Flora, allied now to the opposing court from the one she's tied by blood. By stepping up to be Flora's companion, she's taken a step into the same circle.

She never meant to become a part of this world. Humans aren't supposed to see all this. She lived her whole life up to a few weeks ago not knowing fae were anything other than fairy tales. This world stole her, kidnapped her by the fangs of a vampire. It might have liked for her to never have gotten this far. Now, though, she has a purpose. She has a reason to live. She can see this through.

The unseelie queen claps her hands. The sound causes Vivian to jump, the waves of noise pressing in on her again.

"Good," she says. "It has been decided. Bayler, take Vivian to the back rooms and help her get situated. Flora, you'll take your place and remain here beside us."

A shutter runs through Vivian as her whole name is spoken aloud.

Vivian recoils from a hand on her shoulder, pulling back before realizing it's Flora. "I'll be right behind you," she says, gently guiding Vivian to move past her and behind the thrones.

"I know," Vivian whispers, though there's no way for either of them to really be sure.

Moving past Flora, she locks eyes with Bayler. He starts to speak, then shuts his mouth. Embers flare, deep in the pit of Vivian's stomach. Even just looking at him causes the feeling to rise.

Bayler steps to one side, extending one arm deeper into the shadows behind the throne. Vivian can just make out a singular side door. It would be hidden if it weren't for the two guards posted by either side of it.

As Vivian passes Bayler, he sets a hand lightly on the back of her shoulder blade. She flinches at his touch but keeps walking.

"Don't touch me." Vivian speaks the words through gritted teeth. The seelie fae lifts his hand just far enough that his hand is no longer on his shoulder, but from further away it looks like he's still guiding her. Music rises in volume behind them, the voices of the king and queen of the unseelie fading into the rest of the sounds of their crowd. Two guards detach themselves from their positions and fall in step beside Bayler. Despite his attempts to wave them off discreetly they maintain their position.

"I'm sorry," Bayler says. The words are nowhere near adequate.

They exit the stage, walking down narrow hallways in silence. The walls at least drown out the noise of whatever is happening beyond them. She might not know what she's walking into, but for the moment she can pretend the quiet is a comfort.

The hallway widens. Vivian still doesn't recognize where they are, but she does find her voice. "You left us alone in the dark," she says. Her words are quiet, but build strength as she goes on. "When they locked us in that cell, took each of us to try and win us to their side with promises, you didn't come back. We thought something happened to you. There was no way to know what, but all we could believe was the worst."

Vivian turns over her shoulder, facing him. He looks human, if it weren't for his reddish-brown eyes. "We were waiting for you in the dark, in that cell. But you found your own way out and left us there."

It's more than she meant to say, especially with the knowledge they aren't alone, but the rush of words had to be said. If they had to endure the ceremony of the unseelie court, she will speak her mind now.

"Vivian…"

He hardly gets past the first syllable of her name before she turns on him. The floor-length dress hinders her movement, causing her to stumble, but her hands hit his chest in fists. "Don't say my name again," Vivian says, her voice low. "You're one of them now. You are not my friend."

She can feel the heat in her cheeks. Her breaths quicken, backing up to put space between her and the fae. The two guards begin to close in on her, but Bayler holds up his hands and taking a step back from her.

"Don't touch her, please." The anger in Vivian's eyes doesn't dissipate as the guards listen to him. She's grown from the first time he saw her. She was scared, trembling with her head down too scared to speak. Now she's not afraid to stand face to face with him.

"Please," Bayler says, this time the word pointed toward her. "Let me get you somewhere safe for Flora to meet you. Then..."

"Then you can leave us alone," Vivian says, her voice quieter but with no less emotion behind it.

Bayler nods, emotion flicking across his face too fast for her to read it even if she wanted to. "Then I'll leave you alone."

Vivian steadies herself, trying to regain some sense of posture as she reorients herself down the hallway and begins walking again. It's only a few turns later before the hallway ends at a door. A guard steps around her with a key. It clicks in the lock and swings inward. She can see a small but decorated living area through it. Seating, a table and a desk. It's far from the prison cell she and Flora were acquainted with earlier but it still sends a shiver down her spine. It might be what she asked for, but even while she was in that cell she was never really alone.

Vivian steps inside the room, the train of her dress following her like a shadow. As she starts to turn back around, the door shuts. Panic rises in her chest, tightness spreading through her body.

"Wait!" She rushed back toward the door, almost falling flat on her face. The lock clicks in place just as her hands scrabble for a door handle that's nonexistent. All her hands touch is a lock she can't open from the inside.

"Bayler," she shouts, hating the sound of his name but unsure what else to do. "Bayler!" This time louder, but it doesn't do anything. No one opens the door. There's no voice to reply. Just a consuming silence and the rush of her own heartbeat.

Vivian runs her hand along the whole door, searching for any point of weakness and finding none. All she finds is nail marks in the decorative wood framing, painted over.

"Flora," she whispers, taking a few steps back. Her eyes never leave the door except to glance around the sunlit space around her. "Cass..."

The panic in her chest twists into something like terror, a string around her neck tightening.

"You're looking for something. Is it me? I can tell you my name. I'll let you shout it if you want."

The voice is in her head. Vivian gasps, frantically scanning the room. She knows that voice. She thought she would never have to hear it again, not after her sister freed her. Cassie got her out of that vampire lair, saved her from those fangs. There's no one else physically in the room but she can still hear his voice. He's still her imprint, though that's too kind a word for it. He still has a hold on her.

"Vivian."

It's a mocking, drawn out version of her name. She doesn't want to claim it as her own. Pressure wraps around her body, starting from her gut and wrapping her body in a paralysis only her mind seems to be able to escape.

"No, no, no," Vivian shouts. The dress pools around her as she drops to her knees, eyes squeezed shut with all the force she can muster, hands in her hair and nails digging into her skull. "I told you once to get out. You can't be here."

"You are mine."

There's a possessive tone she can still hear in her nightmares, paired with snake-like eyes and a fanged smile covered with her own blood. The vision causes a wave of nausea.

"You were mine the first time I laid eyes on you, though you didn't know it yet. You should have stayed. They might have taken you from me, but that doesn't change what you are. What I made you to be."

The panic turns to terror, the adrenaline pumping through her body with a force that causes her to shutter. "You have no claim to me," Vivian whispers but she already knows that's not true. He's the only reason she can see this world, the one who kidnapped her from a peaceful life and set her on this path, only…

Hot tears coming down her face, she can finally latch onto Flora's words from before, the last time this happened. He must have been waiting for this moment, waiting for her to slip her focus, ready to pounce.

"Focus on anything else," Vivian whispers, clinging to the fabric of her dress and she bends forward. "Just long enough to force him out, build the wall back up."

"You can't keep me out forever. I will always be able to find you."

Despite his promise verging on a threat, the voice in her head fades. The tension wrapped around her body begins to lose its hold on her.

Cassie saved her from that dark place. She unlocked the door, held her in a hug so long and hard Vivian could have lived in it for the rest of her life. It's only a memory now, but Vivian holds onto that hug with all the strength in her body. Her sister is still here somewhere in the unseelie palace. She's not alone, not as long as they're both alive. If that's all the hope she has to hold on to, if that's enough to silence the vampire trying to get inside her head, then that's more than enough for her.

Vivian sucks in a deep breath, then another. Slowly, carefully she unwinds her hands from the folds of her dress. Despite the layers of fabric there are crescent shapes embedded in her palms. The shimmer of the dress create the illusion of a dream, just a little otherworldly. Tentatively, she feels for the imprint within herself. It's still there. He did something to her she can never undo, but she can't hear him. She can breathe without the force of him crushing the life out of her. There will never be enough distance between them as long as he's still roaming the surface of the earth. Vivian has no doubt of that. The truth of that resounds deep within her bones. But for today, or at least for right now, her body and mind are her own.

She stays there on the floor, just shy of a puddle of fabric, long after both her legs go numb. She stares at the door, willing it to open, but it never does. No matter how many times she mutters Flora's name, her sister's name, everything remains exactly as it is. Vivian's not sure if that's a blessing or a curse. The silence and isolation are her only constant companions, exactly the way she asked for them.